DWARVES

A Short Book of Short Stories

BY

James Gagnon

Illustrations by Carson Wong

SHIPWRECK BOOKS

ISBN: 9781797765204

ACKNOWLEDGMENTS

I'd like to thank everyone who ever sat and actually wrote down anything. It's so exciting and magical and fun to imagine a great story. It's boring, dull work to physically sit and write it all down. Thank you to all the men and women who took the time to put in the work so that I could enjoy their imagination.

More specifically, I'd like to thank my friend, Bear, for reading and critiquing this particular cluster of words. I can read and edit for years, but I'll never see every mistake. Thank you for marking the misspellings and the poor grammar—as well as telling me which parts were a bit crap.

Mr. Carson Wong, my artist. Thank you for being patient as I described images from my mind and then watched you conjure those visions into reality. I have the utmost respect for your talents and look forward to our next project.

Finally, to my wife, Mollie. You are my co-conspirator in everything. This work would be nothing without you. Countless nights of pacing and discussion have brought us here, and I'm looking forward to many, many more. I love you. Always.

LIFE, DEATH, AND TIME

Life was not always in the world. Death waited in the darkness, a glutton, swallowing everything, both the wholesome and the grotesque. And Death grew fat on the demise of the world. He became like a beast, his jaws forever working to devour all things. And if Death was a beast, then Time was his keeper. A tireless worker, Time forever pushed the world towards the jaws of Death. Young or old, rich or poor, strong or weak, Time shepherded all into Death's reach.

The seas turned brown, the soil became as soot, and the sky blackened with clouds and rumbling thunder. The world was dark, and in this darkness, Death was pleased. Time worked endlessly, feeding its pet until Death was unable to move. Still, Time fed the beast, and the glutton ate on. Time would have fed Death the world and everything in it, but it was not to be. While Death sat in the dark, too engorged to seek out his own prey, Life stepped into the world. She saw Death and knew him to be a beast, not capable of understanding. Life also saw Time and knew him to be the cause of the world's demise.

So, Life fought Time. They met where the mountains reached the sky, far from where Death squatted like a toad in the deepest dark. Time was wise and had spent eternity sending all his foes to meet Death. He hid in the shadows, making each attack against his adversary strong and precise. But Life was not afraid of Time, for she did not fear anything, and her quick feet easily dodged his attacks. Life and Time battled, and Death waited. Time grew tired, and Life trapped him there, where the mountains met the sky.

With Time imprisoned, Life moved across the sky, tearing back the clouds and flooding the world with her radiance. She ran through the fields and swam in the oceans, cleansing both with her touch. The world glowing with her essence, Life hunted for Death, determined to close his jaws forever. However, the beast, seeing that Time was no longer his caretaker, had fled to the farthest reaches of the world. Without Time to feed him, Death withered and became as a shadow, with sunken eyes and a deep contempt for Life.

With Death in hiding and Time trapped on the horizon, Life sought to bring beauty to the world where she now dwelt. She planted great gardens and conceived an image of beings that would one day walk among them. Life toiled, and Time watched. Death starved in the coldest dark.

As Life finished her work, Time remained imprisoned on the horizon, and all of her labors were without reward. The world, though full of her essence, did not sprout up with bountiful forests, or echo with the cries of Life's sons and daughters. Time, knowing his place in the world, waited. Life saw her own folly and knew what had to be done. Far away in the darkness, Death feasted on Hope, as the hungry often do.

Life returned to Time, where the mountains meet the sky. She told him of her gardens, planted but not grown. She sang of her children, conceived in her dreams but not yet born. Time listened, knowing he need only wait. Life commanded Time to aid her in populating the world with her conceptions. She promised him freedom if he were to help her. Time then reminded Life of his devotion to Death, a bargain that he dared not break, for even he was afraid of what the beast would do should his hunger not be sated. Being young, Life laughed at Death, hiding away in his hole, and only Time knew of her foolishness.

Life then bargained with Time, and both were pleased. The two left the horizon and made their way through the world, and Time allowed Life to grow and cultivate her gardens and forests. She birthed beings to populate the world, and under Time's watchful gaze, they grew strong and wise in their own right. Life was overjoyed with her new children and laughed as they danced through her gardens, explored her jungles, and swam in her lagoons.

As Life was distracted by her creations, Time sought out Death, and together the pair reforged their alliance. Time told his ally of the children of Life and how they frolicked and laughed without fear of Death. The ravenous beast needed no convincing and immediately began his attacks on the children. Yet, whenever Death sought to devour the children of Life, he found they were as fearless as their mother, and they fought him with the same ferocity.

Frustrated with his new foe, Death sought out Time, and the two struck a bargain. The beast retreated to his cold dark, and Time returned to find Life in her gardens, surrounded by her children. He remained there, and the two were as friends. Time stayed and as he did, the children grew old. With their age came wisdom, and Life was pleased, as this was something she could never give them on her own. She discovered that she loved Time for his gift to her offspring, and when he left the gardens, she allowed some of the oldest and wisest to go with him.

Alas, Time was ever the loyal caretaker of Death, and so he led the first of Life's children to meet the beast in the blackness. There, they were devoured. As he feasted upon the flesh of Life's children, Death laughed, and the cruel sound echoed out of the cold dark and into the warm light of the gardens. Life heard Death and knew that Time had betrayed her. She understood that her children knew Time as their father, and they would surely forever follow him into the cold dark to meet Death and be devoured.

In her sorrow, Life sought out Death, intent on removing him from the world forever. But Time had long since hidden the beast in the deep blackness and Life could not find Death. After searching the world over, Life returned to the gardens to discover that her children still journeyed to the cold dark, as those before them had. Time had taught them well, and now they were his children as well as hers.

The children of Life and Time loved their mother but refused to stay in the garden forever, always yearning to follow the path that their father had shown them. The path into the cold dark. The children had never known fear, but having known their father, they now knew its scent, and they followed it into the black.

Life's sadness and anger turned to bitterness, and she hated Time for leading her children away. Together, they had populated the world with beings of her essence. Now these beings, who used to give her joy, gave her only sorrow and pain. In the heat of her hatred and passion, Life planted a tree, which she hid from Time. Her children cultivated the tree, and under their care it grew quickly. Life sat at the foot of the tree until it consumed her and her malice. Many of her children still followed the pull of Time out of the garden and into the cold dark, but those that stayed and tended to the tree forgot Time and never met Death.

Of all the children of Life and Time, Man was the quickest to become discontent. Even as their mother and father hid themselves away, Mankind sought dominion over the other children. The great tree was not yet fully grown before the first wars began in the farthest reaches of the world. Time allowed Men to send one another to the blackness to greet Death, where the glutton ate all he met, as he had in the days before Life.

But the children of Life were plentiful, and no matter how many followed the call of Time, there were always more. And so, Time continued to lure

his adopted children towards the cold dark, where
Death eventually devoured them, and Life remained
within the great tree where Time held no power.
This was the world after Life stepped into it.

TRUE MAGIC

I

In a world remembered only in dreams, there were two kingdoms. I will begin with the first, as is the best way with stories, and perhaps I will talk of the second at a later time.

There was peace. Not a usual peace—that time between wars that are full of healing wounds and mourning and eventual grumbles and murmurings and unrest. No, this was a True Peace. For over 400 years, a great line of Kings had led their people with keen minds, loving hearts, and unyielding principles. From the Great Eastern Oceans, to the Mountains Unpassable in the Far West. From the Ice Forests of the South, all the way to the Neverending Deserts in the North. One Kingdom. One line of Kings. One True Peace.

It is within this peace that our story begins. I suppose I should give the Kingdom a name, as is the way with tales and such. In honesty, I don't know the True Name, for as I said, this story is remembered only in dreams, and alas, they are not mine. But I will tell the story as best as I can. Whether or not this makes me unfit to tell this tale, I will leave up to your sound judgement. Regardless of what you decide, I will name the Kingdom. From henceforth in our story it will be called Vestal, and it will be most glorious.

The Great Kingdom of Vestal had known War, once upon a time. But while the memories of bloody fields, burning bodies, and broken homes and bones no longer entered the minds of Vestal, the lessons learned from War were carefully handed down through the generations. For these reasons there was the True Army. All men and women of a certain age in Vestal were required to spend a time of their youth protecting the kingdom from the foes of History.

But while the lessons of War were taught in the land, War was not known, and even more extraordinary, neither were the words Hunger nor Poverty. It was a near-Utopian time of harmony. Too good to believe, and perhaps, that is why this is a story and not real life, for in reality, man lacks the ability to live in harmony with one another. If this tale was not a thing of dreams, the Kingdom of Vestal, and the people within it, could not exist. And that would be a shame, because some of them were truly wonderful people.

The most well-known of course, were the Great Kings of Vestal, and with good reason, as they were without question the reason why the kingdom ever knew True Peace. Without them, this dream of harmony would never be, and for that, the Great

Kings deserve names. They are listed here, in the best order I can recall, as it has been many years since this tale first began, and my mind is foggy.

First, there was Jonathan the Victorious, who carried the King's Banner to the farthest reaches of the known world, bringing all Vestal under its shade. Then came Lowlan of Thruss, called the Great Hero of the Last War. The third Great King was named Traam, and though he had lived during the time of War, he had never fought in a battle. Still Traam was much loved and respected as it was he that set the first foundation of the Great Libraries, ratified the Treaty of Equals, and deposed of the last remnants of the Raiders along the Eastern Sea. Without Traam, it is believed that the Realm of Vestal would have never known True Peace, and that is why he has been remembered and loved.

After the first three Great Kings, there were many more, all of whom ruled well. Some stand out, as their names will undoubtedly show. In truth, it is for their names that they are even remembered in this story. There was Greg the Red Bard, Sir Thomas the Lover, and Kloer the Sower of Seeds. King Jun is remembered for the tower he erected on the Eastern Sea, near the Northern Desert, called The Great Jun Lighthouse. Construction was not finished until eighty years and two kings later, under the reign of King Philip, son of King Brunt the Enforcer; still, King Jun is remembered more fondly than Philip, so great was the architecture and planning that went into the building under his instruction.

Afterwards came King Rutle of the Southern Ice Forest, and he was followed by his son, Rallal the Wise. A generic title but an apt one, for Rallal kept the poor fed and content through a time when a great drought claimed the majority of crops for nearly seven years. No simple task, even for a wise man. Upon his abdication of the throne, King Rallal chose a bright, loving fellow by the name of Jarel to rule the kingdom, as was his right.

King Jarel came to be known throughout the vast reaches of Vestal as a mighty swordsman, as he loved to duel for sport, and it is said that he never lost a match. He was tall, with dark skin, and was very beautiful. His looks and his love for the sword brought him many fair suitors, and he chose wisely. Queen Mery, she is called, and is remembered as much for her leadership as for her husband's sharp eyes and quick smile. They are always remembered together, as one could not have been without the other. Jarel's swordplay never would have kept the King's treasury and been able to build the Mighty Ice Harbors of the Southern Oceans. That was his bride, Queen Mery. And it was Mery that sat upon the throne for twenty-two years following her husband's death at the hands of a drunken servant girl. The girl claimed many things of Jarel, but they should not be remembered here, for Queen Mery never would have his name tarnished. She was the First of the Great Queens to rule Vestal, and there were several, however, none were so wise or as beautiful as Mery.

There could be, and in truth once were, many books all filled from cover to cover with the names and accolades of the Great Kings and Queens of Vestal, but this is not one of those books. For to be honest, I have little desire to write about peaceful times. It is in times of peace that man becomes lazy and self-absorbed, and many are unable to even comprehend such things as War, Famine, or Hardship. Still, for our story to begin, one needs to understand how luscious and happy the Kingdom of Vestal had become.

Now, with this understanding we will step into that time of True Peace, that time of beauty and harmony. We will begin just before the time of Magic. Before the coming of the darkness.

II

We have talked of the Kingdom of Vestal and its True Peace, never knowing War, Hunger, or Poverty, yet there was one thing that did plague the realm. Despite all the wisdom and guidance of the Great Kings, a disease seeped into the homes of the Vestian People. It was unstoppable, unforgiving, and unforeseen.

As you may have guessed, if you've read the previous bit, this story isn't going to end happily. But few endings are happy. And those that claim to be are false. The idea of living "happily ever after" is a lie that only makes the reality of life all that much worse. Not all girls grow up to be princesses, and not all boys grow up to be knights in shining armor. In truth, most people never grow up at all, deciding instead to lock their minds away and remain forever children, always right in their ways and rarely utilizing logic or reason. At least, this was so in the Kingdom of Vestal in the latter years of the True Peace. It was a disease of foolish childishness that took root deep in the heart of the realm. At its heart, every realm is made up of people. And the people of Vestal were spoiled rotten.

I'm sure that the people all had names. Most do. However, names are made for remembering, and to be perfectly candid, only a small handful of the people in our story are worth remembering. So, I think it best that we leave the majority of our cast of characters as nameless beings—eating, breathing, laughing, and utterly unimportant. People spending their existence working hard and sharing their joys and struggles with one another in a whirlwind of life. In short, they were boring.

Now, if one of those hard working, loving people was able to move mountains with his mind, or turn herself into a unicorn (or even a bookshelf for that matter) they would most certainly have a name here, and maybe this story would be about them. But they weren't, so it's not. Being average is not noteworthy. Being average isn't special. Luckily for us, there was a young man living in Vestal during the waning years of the True Peace. His name was Max, and in many ways, he was not average.

Not only was Max no average person, he was lucky. Extremely lucky, as it turns out. Firstly, he was healthy—a lucky feat in a time when indoor plumbing didn't involve a flush. Second, he was born the third son of a Great King. In Vestal, the odds of that happening were roughly four hundred eighty-six thousand to one. Lastly, and I believe most importantly, Max had no desire to be average—what some would call, "normal." Rather, he fought it. With every fiber of his heart and soul, he pushed himself to be different. From a very young age, he never liked playing with others and was often found wandering the grounds of the King's Keep, or among the stacks of books in the King's Library, deep in thought.

When he was just six, his mother took him aside and scolded him for his odd behavior.

They'll think you're strange, and no one will like you. You must have people like you to make friends. You don't understand now, but when you're older, you'll realize that you need friends. People to lean on when you're weak. People to talk you through the difficult times. Without others, one is forced to live quite a lonely life, and you wouldn't want that.

Despite his mother's requests against acting "strange," Max embraced his solitude. He didn't want the company of other people, as he had books and nature to keep his mind occupied. To Max, if someone was to dislike him for not being overly social, then they were a poor example of friendship anyway, and it would be best to skip the whole process altogether and just move on. Besides, he had a lot to do.

Even as a child, he had a voracious appetite for knowledge. The day his hunger began, he was just three years old, and his tutor—another way in which he was lucky—informed him that one day he was going to die. The idea of his own mortality troubled the young prince, giving him nightmares for nearly a week. After that, he put his every thought-filled moment to good use, soaking up every bit of knowledge that he possibly could. In Max's young mind, if he was to die one day, then he was determined to experience everything wonderful in the world. Every book in the King's Great Library was available to him, and he put these resources to excellent use.

When Max was nine, he informed his father that he no longer required the services of a tutor, as he had surpassed the elder man's intellect and, therefore, his usefulness. His father, the Great King Lynn, would have advised his son against this decision, but said decision had been delivered by a messenger from the Great Library, was a lengthy affair, rivaling most legal documents that the King had ever seen, and was written in a steady, bold hand. It was also provided in five different languages, two of which the King admittedly didn't recognize. His advisors informed him that one was an ancient, dead language believed to be used by a race of people once native to a remote region of Vestal that was known for its healing hot springs. The second language, none of them recognized at all, but they quickly deduced that it was, in fact, a new language that Max had crafted himself.

The tutor was let go, and at the age of nine, Max was finally able to make his own way in the world. For the most part, he ignored his mother's advice. Frankly, he disagreed with her logic. It was her belief that a life spent without others was lonely, and Max was anything but lonely. He knew every animal, vegetable, and mineral in the known world by name. In his books, he had mined more knowledge than most people could have done in a dozen lifetimes. He read at least one volume a day, remembering nearly every written word, and could quote the interesting bits verbatim.

When he was ten, he left the library and made a sort of personal pilgrimage to the Great Jun Lighthouse, on the Eastern Sea, which boasted the greatest view in all Vestal. However, while most studied the sea's horizon or the endless reaches of the Northern Desert, Max used the opportunity to study what was directly over his head. He had read about the stars and their patterns in the oldest volumes of the Great Library, but now he studied their movements, colors, and brightness. He wrote down everything he observed, and when he returned to the King's Keep over a year later, he had filled nearly fifty books with drawings and text. These books he added to the Great Library and then promptly attacked the study of anatomy with the same vigor and poise as he had astronomy.

It was only after two of his brothers discovered him dissecting the body of an old doorman in the basement of the Western Tower that anyone dared halt Max's quest for knowledge. He was summoned before his father to explain himself, which he did. The doorman had already been dead, having slipped and fallen down the stairs just hours before.

When questioned about his hiding the body away in the Western Tower, Max stated that it was the coldest place in the Keep, and therefore, the best place to keep a body fresh.

Why didn't he tell anyone about finding the body? They would have stopped him from taking it.

Why desecrate the corpse rather than give the man a proper burial? Dissection was not desecration, and the man was doing more good for the betterment of mankind than he ever had done whilst alive.

What punishment should he be given? None. He had done no wrong.

What should be done with him then? He should be left alone with his studies, as he had much to do and the doorman was ripening by the minute.

By the time he was twelve, Max had a firm grasp of the inner working of the human body, and no one in the Keep dared go anywhere near the Western Tower. The young prince adopted the Tower as his own and began to transform the building into his dedicated personal space. The basement was outfitted for experimentation, whether that meant discovering how long it took for milk to sour or the exact weight of a fruit fly. The middle rooms were made into Max's personal library. In size, it was nothing in comparison to the King's Library, but the quality and content of these books more than made up for their smaller number. Many were written by Max himself, a fact that he took no pride in, as he was too busy to be proud.

His thirteenth birthday found Max quite knowledgeable. From the mannerisms of every known migratory bird, to the proper equations used to track the motions of the stars, he was a master on nearly every conceivable topic. He had single-handedly produced more books than any other author, be them philosopher, poet, or scientist. Not only had he produced his own books, but he had read and memorized thousands of other written works. He knew the names and tales of every notable person since the Last War. He could sing, recite poetry, and even speak to various birds and beasts.

Now, to you and I, this might all sound amazing and even somewhat unbelievable. But to Max, on the day before his thirteenth birthday, it worried him. He had studied for nearly ten years, always with a ferocious energy that would have concerned his friends, if he had had any. His father, King Lynn was far too busy keeping the realm at peace to notice that one of his sons was so strange. His mother was too worried that he might embarrass the family name to even be seen with her own son. And his brothers and sisters made no attempt to hide their thoughts about their unordinary sibling.

For the first time in his young, full life, Max was scared. Not the kind of scared one gets when a cat darts out of the night shadows with a hiss, or the feeling of horror that creeps upon certain people when out in stormy water in a small boat or high atop a mountain with treacherous footing. This was a deep fear, dark and brooding. For the first time in his life, Max was bored. He had learned everything that there was to learn, to the best of his expansive knowledge. Now, with nothing left to learn, he was just an observer. He could predict the weather, the movement of the stars, and even the actions of most people, given the right information. For while he didn't enjoy the company of people, he had still studied them all his life, and he found them, on the whole, to be stupid, boring, and altogether dull.

When one is able to predict the future, even to the slightest degree, everyday life can become tedious. All of Max's studies and personal experience, however limited the latter might be, had taught him as much. On the eve of his thirteenth birthday, sitting in his Library in the Western Tower, the young prince came to believe that he had, in fact, learned everything he wished to know about the world and its inhabitants. The idea made him so afraid that he sat by the fire and rocked back and forth for nearly a quarter of an hour before he realized his next course of action.

Just as he had refused to be average at the age of three, Max now refused to be bored for the rest of his life. In the time of True Peace in Vestal, a man of his position could easily live to be seventy, and he balked at the idea of living with such boredom for the next sixty-odd years.

So, after almost a full half-hour of introspective thought by the fire, Max decided to end his suffering. He would end his young life before it had the chance to get dull. He had read several texts that probed at the idea of a life after death, but he forced the memory of those texts from his mind, shuddering at the thought of another miserable existence after this one. Instead, he hurried to his basement laboratory, gathered up a long coil of rope he had once used to tie down a horse during a rather horrific surgery, and hurried back up the cold stone stairs, past the library, to the top floor of the tower.

I feel as though I must pause for a brief moment and offer some perspective. The idea to end one's life comes to many people, especially when we are young. Decisions made in the heat of the moment are often not well thought out. Now, while Max *did* think the idea over, weighing the pros and the cons against one another in his little mind, there is no way that he could have made a *wise* decision. Although the young Prince was one of the most knowledgeable people in the kingdom, wisdom only comes with age and time.

In short, deciding to kill himself was the most childish thing the boy had ever done.

Max threw open the large, shuttered window of the study and busied himself by tying one end of the rope around a rafter up near the ceiling. The knots took him a moment to get right, as he had studied how they were supposed to be tied but had never actually put the knowledge to practical use. Still, within a few minutes, he had one end of the rope fastened around the roof's center beam and the other tied about his neck in a traditional hangman's noose. He had decided that hanging himself inside the top of the tower could be tricky, as his small frame might not have enough weight to snap his neck, and he would be left choking to death, legs kicking. On the other hand, he didn't want to merely jump out of the window, as there was the slim possibility that the fall might only maim him, and the last thing he wanted to do was spend the rest of his horrid, boring life as a cripple. So, he decided that it was best to leap with a good length of rope, so that when the line did go tight, he would be falling fast enough that his neck would surely break, and death would come quickly.

When all was ready, Max stood on the window sill, hands braced on the outside of the large frame, the rope around his neck. Seventy feet below, in the courtyard of the King's Keep, it was already dark as the servants and royalty readied themselves for the prince's birthday celebrations the following day. Yet, up above them all, braced in the tower window, Max had a clear view of a sunset most beautiful. He looked at the sun one last time and wished he cared how beautiful it was.

Then, he closed his eyes, took a deep breath, and stepped out of the window.

III

"Oh my! You're really gonna do it?"

Max's eyes flew open, his body jolting awkwardly as his subconscious survival instincts kicked in, sending his arms flailing backwards to catch the windowsill. His torso twisted about, and he caught himself, just barely. He found himself in an awkward position for a terrifying moment, a forearm and most of his left leg hooked safely over the sill, his remaining limbs clawing madly in an attempt to bring the rest of his body and the tangle of rope back inside the tower's upper room.

Thirty seconds of panicked scrambling and Max was back in the sanctuary, his heart palpitating and his feet suddenly sweating. After a few deep breaths, he whirled about, his eyes seeking the source of the voice that had halted his hastily developed suicide attempt.

The room was empty. Well, not empty. The room was actually quite a comfortable study area, complete with armchair, woven rug, and a low table all set before the fireplace. It was Max's favorite place in the world he realized, and the thought gave him momentary pause before he deduced that the voice he had heard must have come from outside the window.

He approached slowly, peering cautiously over the sill at first, then moving closer and poking his head through the large opening, his eyes darting madly about the tower's dark, stone exterior.

"Change your mind?"

Max jerked his head away from the sound, cracking the side of his jaw on the bottom of the sill. The sudden pain melted his trepidation, and with a grunt, he once more returned to the window, his hands braced against the inside of the wooden sill, his head cocked to the side, neck straining as he looked upwards, to the eave of the roof and the source of the voice.

A pair of brown eyes met his. A round nose, with a cluster of clever, dirty fingers under it, all clinging to the lip of the overhang. The eyes and nose shifted, revealing a soft mouth that opened as a strand of hair, long and loose, tumbled softly toward him.

"Would you mind taking the rope from around your neck? Hang yourself with me here, they'll think I had something to do with it. And I didn't, so I'm not having you stand there with a rope around your neck."

Max discovered his hands were cold and clammy as he hastily untied the hangman's knot, his mouth suddenly dry. Why was he nervous? He was never nervous. It didn't suit his character, and he didn't have time for such foolishness. Still, for the first time in his young, newly saved life, he was very worried. It was something about the voice. It was quick, almost demanding, and he found it warmly aloof, a combination that should not exist, yet somehow did.

He freed himself from the rope, and as it fell to the floor, he looked back to the window in time to observe a pair of grimy, bare feet alighting on the sill. Max watched, frozen in his own sanctuary, as a lanky-framed girl carefully lowered herself from the roof above with an almost natural grace. Despite her starved frame and unwashed appearance, she moved like a dancer, stepping from the sill and into the top room of the Western Tower.

"Oh, this is actually quite cozy!"

The young girl flitted quickly past Max and into the belly of the room, first running a hand across the back of his armchair and then moving to inspect an old tapestry on the far wall. It was nearly two hundred years old and depicted a green meadow with a duo of rabbits silhouetted by a setting sun. The master work of art had gilded edges, and golden thread showed highlights throughout the image, but Max knew it was the name of the artist that made the old piece priceless.

The girl sniffed loudly, wiping a hand across her nose and then on the hem of her coarse, wool dress. She turned, and Max saw a kindness in her eyes, a smile on her lips.

"Do you keep children locked up in the basement?"

Max licked his lips, his mind racing to understand the question that his mouth was already trying to answer.

"Wha...? I don—"

Her smile turned into a chuckle, her hands shooting upwards in a vain attempt to hide her obvious merriment.

"Oh, come on! Surely you know what they all say about you? That you kidnap children and cook them in a large pot in the basement of the tower? That you live here, and not in the Inner Keep, because your mother won't live under the same roof as a cannibal?"

Max was suddenly aware that his mouth was open. He closed it and forced himself to swallow as he straightened his back and absently kicked the rope out from beneath his feet, arranging his thoughts as he began to defend against this invasion of privacy.

"I don't know what you've heard, exactly—but there is nothing of that sort going on here. Now, I must insist that you go."

The girl's laughter stopped, her mouth suddenly a tight line, and for a moment, Max found himself thinking he might have offended her. Then he spotted a glint in her eyes, and she shook her head, the smile creeping back into the corner of her lip.

"No. I don't believe you. You have to prove it. Prove that you don't have anything to hide and only then will I be on my way."

He opened his mouth again, intent to win her over with logic, but she was already in motion, her light body bounding across the room, past the furniture to the head of the stairwell. She paused momentarily on the top step, shooting him a quick smirk.

"I mean, do you expect me to climb back out the window?"

She laughed aloud at his blank expression and then disappeared to the floors below. Max scurried after her, half entranced, half concerned. He had never had anyone else inside his tower, not since the King's carpenters had finished their work on the abode a year prior. Max looked after himself, and therefore, required no servants. The idea of another person intruding on his privacy made his feet move rapidly down the stairwell, nearly causing him to trip.

The strange girl fluttered from the stairs to the bookcase to the desk and about the entire living area like a bird, commenting on each thing her hands touched. The books were *lovely*, the desk was *tidy*, and the candles were *a bit plain.* Max followed in her wake, at first intent to fix any damage she caused. But the girl's light step and soft touch left the room undisturbed. She abandoned the living quarters that made up the bulk of the tower's interior and continued her hurricane of observation. She passed the main door to the courtyard, moving instead to the small door in the darkest corner of the tower.

"And *what* do you keep behind there?"

Max practically had to throw himself against the door to halt the girl's advance.

"No need to go down there. You've seen enough! I must ask that you turn around and see yourself out."

He nodded as he said this, indicating with his eyes that she leave via the main entrance. As he looked back to her, she was slowly moving toward him, slinking like a thin alley cat, a playful smile crossing her eyes.

"Oh? You're asking me now? A moment ago, you were insisting..."

Max felt his back bump into the door as the girl came within a foot of him. He had never been this close to a girl. She smelled of tree sap and fresh air, sunlight and warm afternoons. He cleared his throat.

"Then... I *insist.*"

She stepped back, as though his words had cut her. The smile melted away, her eyes widening. The playfulness disappeared, her body suddenly arching away, back stiffening.

"You really don't want me to see what's down there... do you? You *do* keep bodies in the basement!

And here I thought you were just a misunderstood boy, without any friends..."

Her abrupt shift from confident to fearful tugged at something in Max's stomach. He stepped away from the door, his hands and head shaking back and forth as he fought quickly to explain.

"No! It's not that! I don't have any bodies... well, that is to say, I don't have any *human* bodies down there... Rats! It's the rats! They're all over the place, and I wouldn't want you to get bitten or... startled."

She continued to back away slowly, her body tense, like a deer readying itself to escape a pack of encroaching dogs. She licked her lips.

"So... you don't take children from their cribs and drink their blood down in your lair? Or cut out the tongues of virgins to use in a soup?"

Max fought to retain his composure. The idea that he would steal a child from its bed was ridiculous. This girl had just heard some stupid rumor, and now he actually had to address it. It was, for the young scholar, a low point in his interactions with other people, not that there had been many high points. Still, his shoulders sagged a bit as he let out a long, frustrated sigh.

"No, I'm not a cannibal. I would never dream of hurting a child, let alone dining on its—"

He was cut off as the girl suddenly darted past him, grasped the latch, and threw open the door. Having lured him away from the basement entrance, she was now smiling once again, her tone playful.

"Well, I suppose in that case, I've nothing to fear, do I?"

He stepped forward, his hands reaching out, his tongue fumbling for an answer to her rhetorical question. But she was already disappearing down into the musty depths of the tower, a giggle echoing back up the stone stairs as she went.

Max, defeated in what he now realized had been a game, trudged after her, making sure to close the door behind him before he descended into the depths of the tower.

By the time he reached the base of the stairs, Max had lost sight of the girl, but he could hear her voice. She called back to him, her voice somewhat hollowed by the low ceiling. Max made his way to the center of the great, round room and stood by his worktable. The girl circled, asking questions. The boy remained motionless, giving answers.

What do you do down here? Research. *What kind of research?* All kinds. *What is this?* A map of blood flow through the body of a mouse. *Why make a map of that?* I wanted to and it was an interesting afternoon. *What's in these bottles?* Dirt samples. *Where is the dirt from?* All over the kingdom. *Have you been all over the kingdom?* Yes. *What's it like?* Dull. *Then why go?* To get dirt samples.

At length, the girl appeared from behind a rack of shelving, her eyes still darting from one pile of oddities to the next. She stalked up to the center workbench, taking up a position opposite him. She planted her hands on the tabletop, her attention suddenly focused on the boy.

"And *where...* are all the rats?"

Max opened his mouth to answer but then remembered that he'd lied about rats in the basement. He wished he hadn't lied to her, even over such a small, trivial thing, and that wish was altogether unfamiliar to the young prince. He closed his mouth, his eyes locked with hers. She was unflinching. Though just a girl, no older than he, she held her ground like one of the King's Guard, face taut with hidden emotion, eyes forcibly cold. The quiet of the moment was choking him, and he wished again that he'd never said that there were rats in the basement.

Then she laughed. Max had never heard anything so sweet. His chest exploded with warmth as he realized she was only feigning seriousness. The knot in his stomach disappeared. His cheeks burned and he found himself smiling, something he wasn't prone to do. He was happy. Happy she didn't care that he had lied about the rats, happy she was laughing, happy she was there.

The girl's laughter died, but her smile remained. Max swallowed, opened his mouth to speak but was abruptly cut off as she started back toward the stairs. She called over her shoulder to him as she moved.

"You're not as bad as people say, Max. I'm glad you didn't end up jumping out of that window."

Max had turned to follow her but froze momentarily as he remembered that he had nearly jumped out a window less than a quarter of an hour before. There was something that surprised him even more. He was *glad* that she had saved him. The sound of the door latch at the top of the stairs jolted him out of his trance, and he scrambled up the stairwell after her. He arrived at the top just in time to see the girl skipping toward the tower's main door.

"Wait!"

He winced at the sound of his voice as he squeaked out the single word. Still, despite his embarrassment, his plea had the desired effect. The girl stopped and looked at him, her hand on the large brass knob of the door.

"Yes?"

He was suddenly worried. Worried that she would think he was boring, that he was wasting her time, that he was silly. He fumbled for something to say—some way to convince her he wasn't a crazy person who lied about rats. He said the first thing that came to his mind, and he immediately regretted it.

"How did you know my name is Max?"

She laughed, her hand turning the knob and opening the door.

"You're a prince of the True King, Max. Everyone knows your name."

She turned to leave, the door squeaking slightly. Suddenly, Max realized what he wanted to say, what he wanted to know more than anything else in the world. He nearly yelled out the question as she began to disappear through the doorway and into the night.

"What's your name?"

There was a brief pause, then the girl's head and shoulder appeared as she leaned back inside the doorway.

"Samantha. But don't call me that. Call me Sam."

He took a step forward, not wanting the conversation to end.

"Is that what your friends call you?"

Sam laughed again, and Max was happy. She shook her head, the laugh dying to a chuckle as she disappeared into the night.

"And what makes you think I have friends, Max?"

The door closed behind her, and Max was once again alone in his tower. But for the first time in his life, he didn't feel alone. Her name was Sam, and she was anything but average.

IV

The next day was Max's thirteenth birthday. He tolerated the celebration well enough. The whole affair was ridiculous, as the young prince didn't even want to be there, and it was his educated guess that no one else did either. It was all pomp and ceremony, and he made a mental note to tell his father that he wouldn't be attending next year. The matter was of little importance at present, as he had a much bigger problem to deal with.

Ever since Sam had climbed through the top window of the tower, Max's mind had been like a boat out on the sea in a thick fog. For the first time since he was three, he couldn't think clearly, and this problem held his complete attention. As his birthday wore on, a feast took place in the King's Hall. Max took little notice of the festivities. The jugglers, fire-breathers, and dancing raccoons all seemed to fade away as the young prince tried to figure out what was clouding his mind.

As he sat in the King's Hall, a whirlwind of feasting and drinking about him, Max looked through the large, arched window on the Western side of the room. He gazed past the inner wall, over the tops of various outer buildings, all the way to the far edge of the castle. The Western Tower loomed over the entire view like a scar, the top window forever a reminder of his stupid attempt to kill himself. But that wasn't what was bothering him. The window also reminded him of the girl, of Sam.

Everything about her seemed a mystery, an enigma that he couldn't wait to solve. She wasn't intimidated by him, or his admittedly strange ways, but rather, she was curious. She had asked him many questions, which meant she wanted to know more about him. That very idea made him keep scanning the top of the Western Tower, hoping to see her lanky figure appear, but it didn't. He wanted to know more about her too. In fact, he had a list of questions that he wanted to ask.

Last night, after re-coiling the rope and packing it away in the basement, Max had paced a circle around the table in the sanctuary of the tower's top floor. At length, he had retrieved ink and parchment, sat down written out a list of things to ask Sam. Just in case he should see her again.

The list started off simply enough, but as it went on, and Max thought more and more of the gaunt girl in the dirty dress, his questions began to grow more abstract.

> *Where are you from?*
> *How old are you?*
> *Why were you on the roof?*
> *Were you spying on me?*
> *Who told you that I eat children?*
> *Did you really believe that I ate children?*

Why are you not scared of me?
Are you scared of anything?
Have you ever been to the Eastern Sea?
Would you go to the Eastern Sea?
How can someone like you not have any friends?

Max had written the list, read it over several times and then burned it, cursing his childishness as the flame consumed his curiosity. If Sam ever saw a list like that, she would think he was just a silly, average boy and would never talk to him again. And he needed to talk to her again. He had never wanted friends before, probably because his siblings had friends, and they were all dreadfully boring. Sam was anything but boring, and she had said she didn't have any friends. If they were to become friends, then he could ask her all the questions he wanted, and she couldn't make fun of him, because they would be friends. At least, he was pretty sure that's how friendship worked.

With no end to the overelaborate birthday celebrations in sight, Max found an acceptable reason to excuse himself. He told his father that the dinner had given him terrible bowel discomfort. Great King Lynn gave his weird son a long blank stare before nodding his approval. Max ducked out the Great Hall's back exit, and no one missed him.

He headed toward his tower, and as he moved he had to keep slowing his pace, as his limbs seemed to want to run the whole way. He wanted to get back to the tower, to the sanctuary of the top floor. He could wait by the window, maybe Sam would come back and visit him. If she didn't, he could always go to the King's Guard and ask them to search the city for her. No, that was weird. The fastest way to have a girl not be your friend is to have her hunted down like wild animal. Hunting her down was out of the question. The only logical response was to go to where he'd first seen her, then wait until she came back. He'd read that was how trappers in the Far South caught prey. They used bait to bring the animals into the traps. What could he use as bait? Maybe some sweetcake? Sam was thin, but she was a person, and people got hungry. He would bring sweetcakes to the top of the tower and wait for her to return. Logical.

It was only after returning to the Western Tower and setting out sweetcake and tea, that Max realized his stupidity. Rather than ordering the Guards to hunt a girl down like a dog, he was going to try to lure her into some sort of trap using sweetcake as bait. The young prince cursed himself, sat down in his armchair, and for the first time ever, he wished he was normal.

Crazy hunter or logical thinker, either way, Max waited in his upper sanctum for the girl to reappear. The sun went down, so he lit a few lamps and stoked the fire to ward off the cold provided by the large Westerly window, which he had left open. The night air brought a chill, so Max changed into his silken pajamas, donned a pair of fur slippers, and wrapped himself in a blanket. The young prince settled down by the fire with a mug of tea and a book called *A History of the Southern Tribal Monks of the First Century of True Peace*. A bit of light reading while he kept an eye on the window and the clock on the wall. More than once the long hand moved past the twelve, and Max would stoke the fire and refill his mug.

The cold air continued to blow in through the window, and Max burrowed farther under the blanket, peering at the clock sourly, his eyes fighting to stay open. The fire popped, crackled, and spat a few sparks out on the hearth. Max tried with all his might to focus on the passage in front of his eyes, to consume what they meant, but he found himself re-reading the same passage over and over, his mind wandering in a fog. He had read the phrase "*practice and meditation give the mind power to change its properties*" nearly ten times, and he still had no idea what it meant. His eyes closed, his head rested on the back of the armchair, and his hand gradually loosened its grip on the book.

Max awoke as the book slipped off his lap and knocked into the table, which in turn jostled his mug, splashing tea. As he moved to clear the mess, he heard a rustling by the window, and he turned to see that it was now raining in through the great opening. He moved to the edge of the sill, gave a quick glance up at the eve of the roof, and then closed the shutters. Sam wasn't coming tonight. He pictured, briefly, the coil of rope in the basement, then pushed aside the thought as he realized that the tea had spilled on the pages of his book as well as the table. The boy shrugged off the blanket from around his shoulders and darted forward, muttering angrily at his own negligence and silliness. There had been honey in the tea, and now the pages would stick together. He quickly and carefully gathered up the old tome and shuffled down the stairs to the tower's main living area.

As Max stood by the washbasin in his silken pajamas and fur slippers, carefully dabbing at the book with a wet rag, he heard a tapping sound coming from somewhere behind him. He stopped fussing over the book a moment and listened. He heard the rain coming down and a rumble in the distance, but the rapping had ceased. He returned to his task, forgetting the wet rag, choosing instead to blow on the pages and hope they dried well. Again, there was a tapping, this time much more forceful, as though someone were knock—

Max dropped the book and practically ran to the front door. He paused for a moment, still unsure whether he had imagined the sound. Then, there was a muffled cry from the other side of the heavy door, which now visibly shook as someone kicked the outside planks. The young prince unbolted the door and was immediately shoved aside as Sam forced her way into the room. Max bolted the door, securing them both within the tower and away from the elements.

He turned to greet her, but the girl had already vanished from the dimly lit main living area, her shadow bounding up stairs toward the glow of the fire and lamps on the floor above. Max noticed that she had tracked in mud, and a good deal of water puddled up in front of the door. He thought to get a mop, then decided that the floor could wait. Sam was here, and he needed to ask her his questions.

He was halfway up the long, curving staircase, his feet slipping on the newly wet stone, before he thought to fetch a towel for the girl. No matter how cozy it was up in his study, there was no replacement for a warm towel after being soaked and chilled to the bone. A few moments later and Max was once again moving quickly up the stairs, a towel and clean bathrobe tucked under his right arm, a large plate with a few fresh sweetcakes and a bit of butter balanced in his left hand.

The upper sanctum was bathed with gentle, glowing light. Delicate shadows lapped and played gently at the far edges of the room. But it was to the center of the room that Max gave his attention. The girl stood, soaking in the warmth of his holy sanctum. Her hair clung in long, wet tangles, like seaweed on the—

"Are you going to give me that towel? Because right now, you're just standing there staring, and it's starting to freak me out."

Max *had* been staring, and he tried to hide his face by looking at his feet as he moved across to the low table, setting the plate of cakes down before offering her the towel, which she promptly tugged out of his grip. As he placed the robe on the back of the armchair, he cleared his throat, before giving a silly explanation.

"I wasn't sure that I'd brought enough... cakes."

Sam chuckled, the sound melting into the room as warmly as the light of the fire.

"I should think you've got enough. There must be a score of sweetcakes on those plates. Then again, one can never have too many sweetcakes, I suppose."

She laughed aloud, and in that moment, as Sam stood toweling dirt and rainwater from her hair, Max was sure that she was the most perfect person he'd ever met. He nearly thought this out loud, but luckily, he caught himself. For a few moments, he tried to remember the list of questions he wanted to ask, but he eventually gave up. All his previous intentions were lost in this moment, in the warmth and quiet of his study. The young prince quickly thought of a new question and once again winced—regretting it almost immediately.

"Why are you here?"

Sam stopped off drying her hair for a moment, cocking an eyebrow, a frown on her lips.

"Should I not be? I thought you'd be okay."

Max cut her off, his voice a mousy squeak.

"No! That's not how I meant it! You're fine. I just meant it like—I don't know. I'm glad you're here, I was just wondering if there's a particular *reason* that you're here."

Sam laughed. Whether at his stammering, or just because she was a pleasant person, Max didn't care.

"Well, I figured I'd pop round just because we're friends..."

She paused and deposited the towel on the floor. It was covered with grime and wet dirt, and Max made the mental note to throw it away once she was gone. Had she just said they were friends? Max made a mental note of that too. She reached for the robe, froze for a second, and then promptly stripped out of her dirty, wet dress. She now stood, naked for a brief moment as she snatched the robe from the chair. She was naked, and they were friends. Max's mouth was as dry as the Northern Desert as Sam continued her thought, unconcerned.

"...but if you need an excuse for me to be here, I suppose I'm here because it's your birthday. I figured I'd stop by and give you a present."

She finished tying the robe's cord about her waist and began fishing her hair out from beneath her collar. Max had never been so frightened. The girl moved toward him, and his heart threatened to stop altogether. She was nearly on him now, her feet sinking into the softness of the carpet, bare legs still streaked with dirt. Max held his ground, and the moment stretched into something of an eternity.

Then she was on her hands and knees, her head shoved up against the side of the armchair, a strained look on her face as she fished underneath the furniture with her right arm. A moment later, and she was up, displaying the young prince's gift with pride.

"His name is George. At least, that's what I've called him. He's a bit scrawny, but he's a tough old sod. I saw him wandering about, and I thought, '*Every Magician needs a pet!*' Maybe he'll even be able to take care of those rats in the basement!"

Sam held the nastiest animal Max had ever seen. He'd dissected better looking cats. It probably had lice, worms, and a skin rash, but these were the least of Max's problems. The young prince blinked slowly, letting the girl's words sink in for a moment. She obviously wanted to him to be excited about her gift, but he was still hung up on the other bit.

"Magician?"

The word stuck in his throat. He needed a drink of water, tea, anything. Sam laughed aloud, attempting to wrap both herself and the cat in the blanket Max had left on the floor earlier.

"Yes! I mean, you could say wizard or mage. Well, not mage. That sounds a bit violent. I like Magician the best. After all, the word 'Magic' is right in there. And it just fits—like from the stories! And, like the stories, every Magician needs a pet. Some have toads, spiders, or bats, but I thought none of those were really fitting for a Magician who is the son of the True King, so I—"

Max cut her off.

"Magic? Like, Fairies? Flying carpets? Men rising from the dead? All that?"

There was a harsh quiet in the upper room as Sam stooped, depositing 'George' on the floor where he fled with a slight limp to the shadows beneath the armchair. She believed in fairies, gnomes, and the tales told by nurses to little babies. The fog that had invaded Max's mind was starting to clear, and he was suddenly aware she was just a child. His expression must have said as much, because Sam was no longer meeting his gaze.

"Well, I don't know about all that, but you do fit all the characteristics of a Magician."

He was confident.

"Yes, but Magic d—"

Now she cut him off, meeting his gaze with a twinkling fire in her eyes.

"Shall we go down the list?"

List? His list? No, he'd burnt that up in the fire last night. Max winced as his voice broke yet again.

"List?"

The lanky girl moved swiftly to sit cross-legged on the floor opposite the armchair, her back to the fire. She made a great show of rolling her eyes as she brushed at her wet, tangled hair with her bony fingers.

"You live alone and you don't have any friends. There's vats of dead frogs in the *laboratory* in your basement. Plus, you have loads of books! I bet you were reading a book just now—weren't you?"

Max nodded.

"I was..."

Sam grabbed a sweetcake from the plate and took a huge bite off of one corner as she reached for the tea kettle.

"And? What was it called?"

Max blinked. She was serious. She actually believed what she was saying. Unless this was another joke, but there was a sharp hook in Max's stomach that told him Sam wasn't joking. Joke or not, he decided to play along.

"It was called *A History of the Southern Tribal Monks of the First Century of True Peace*, but tha—"

Max was sure that Sam's laughter would have been heard across the kingdom had her mouth not been crammed with sweetcake. The muffled sound turned to a choking cough as the skinny girl inhaled some of the food. The young prince didn't move, choosing to wait patiently for her to take a sip of tea and cleared her throat. When she did, she laughed, but it was a bit forced, more to make a point than out of genuine mirth.

"So, you're reading ancient books about tribal monks, in your tower, above your laboratory?"

It was the boy's turn to roll his eyes.

"You keep bringing up the lab! It's for scientific research and in no way points to the fact that I'm a Magician or that magic even exists... Which it doesn't."

He'd added the end bit just as Sam had opened her mouth to speak. He never found out what she was going to say, as she chose instead to close her mouth and pour more tea. She was thinking. He could see the light in her eyes, and it unnerved him. Crossing the room, Max stoked the fire, placing a large chunk of wood atop a bed of hot coals. Something told him that wherever this conversation was going, the girl was now in charge. She was obviously a free spirit, maybe even a Looney. His best course of action was to wait for her response, then counter with logic. If she didn't respond to that, he could always call the guards as a last resort. The young prince turned and moved cautiously to sit down in the armchair across from Sam, who rested with her back to the fire.

Neither spoke for a few minutes. Max heard the rain brushing across the roof as the wind rattled the shutters. The fire cracked and popped. The clock on the wall was showing that the time was well past midnight, but the boy was no longer tired. He had spent the evening dreaming for this girl to show up, but now that she was here, he couldn't wait for her to be gone. At least, he thought he wanted her gone. He pictured the room without her in it, and he suddenly changed his mind. He didn't want Sam to go, but he didn't want her telling him that he was something out of a children's story. That was... well, childish.

"You think I'm silly, don't you? Or crazy, maybe?"

Sam's question caught Max off his guard. Indeed, her voice had made him startle slightly, as his mind was deep in thought. For a moment, he hesitated, not sure how to answer. She was the closest thing to a friend that he'd ever had. In fact, she was the only person he'd ever wanted as a friend. He didn't want her to leave, but he wasn't about to lie to her, as that wouldn't help the situation. Also, lying about the truth wasn't something Max did well.

"Yes."

He said the word plainly, flatly.

"Yes to which? Crazy or silly?"

Max shrugged his shoulders ever so slightly, the hint of a smile tugging at the corner of his lip.

"They're pretty much the same thing, really. When you're young, people call you silly, but when you're old, it's called crazy. Depends on how old you are, I guess."

Max was relieved to see the girl across from him give a soft smile.

"Is that your way of asking how old I am?"

The young prince took a moment before answering. The question seemed simple, but there was a look in her eye—a sharp light, like the reflection of the sun flashing off a mirror. She might be crazy, but she was most definitely smart. Her expression told Max that she had an idea, some mental pitfall she expected in the upcoming conversation that he'd not yet seen. He wasn't afraid but, rather, challenged.

"Yes. Yes, I suppose that is my way of asking you your age."

Sam smiled, showing her teeth, and the look told Max that he'd just stepped right into her snare. The girl downed her second mug of tea and refilled it from the kettle. She was practically beaming with delight as she set about negotiating the conversation's next step.

"How about we make a deal? You ask a question, and then I'll ask a question. That way, we both get to know one another, and we both get answers. You can choose not to answer a question but only once. Deal?"

This was a game. Max didn't like games, but she was obviously intent on playing. He'd go along but not by her rules.

"Alright. But I go first, and my question about your age doesn't count."

Sam nodded slowly, her eyes narrowing.

"Oh, choosing your questions carefully? That's fine. I've got nothing to hide from you."

She was right, Max was choosing carefully. Her age could wait. He wanted to know more pressing things.

"Are you an orphan?"

Sam didn't so much as blink.

"Yes, I am. There's your answer. Now, my turn. Have you ever kissed a girl?"

Max suddenly felt the heat from the fire, sweat breaking out on his forehead and palms. He licked his lips, pulling his eyes quickly away from hers and looked about the table for his own tea mug. His mind was on the defensive, twisting to evade her probing awkwardness.

"No—That's not fair! I—What?!"

Sam's arm shot upward, one of her long, bony fingers pointing to his mouth. There was another laugh as she exclaimed;

"Ha! You asked, "What?" That's a question! I'll answer it, and then ask another of my own!"

Max bit his lip as he found his mug and began to fidget with the teabox. This game was silly. It was a silly, stupid game that he was losing.

"Not really fair..."

She straightened up, grabbing another sweetcake and taking a serious tone.

"Doesn't matter! The rules are the rules. I'll answer your question by repeating my first; Have you ever kissed a girl? Now, I'll ask my second question; Can you prove that magic doesn't exist?"

The boy's eyes shifted away from the girl's sly smile, choosing to stare at the hearth as he saw the paradox he was in. He watched the mangy cat pull itself out from under the chair and climb up onto the hearth as Sam re-explained the rules of her silly game to him.

"Remember, you can only give me one answer, and you can pass only once. If you answer one question, that means that you refuse to answer the other. So, either tell me if you've kissed a girl, or tell me if you can prove that magic doesn't exist."

Max glared a hole into the back of the cat's skull as it lifted a long rear leg straight in the air over its head and began tidying itself. *George*. What had *George* done to deserve such a name? This girl was silly. Almost as silly as he was. Why had he let her in? The game wasn't fair. But he was not one to duck the rules. He had to answer but which question?

Sam was smiling.

"Well, I don't know how many girls you've been around, but you seemed awfully sure that magic didn't exist..."

So, it was clear to him now. He'd been outplayed, and they both knew it. He wasn't about to tell her that he'd never kissed a girl. He would have to answer the other question. Could he *prove* that magic didn't exist? To say 'No' would mean that it, in fact, could exist, and she would be right. But if he said 'Yes', he might be forced to somehow back up his answer. He might actually have to try to prove magic didn't exist. The very idea made his scholarly pride hurt.

"Time's up! You've got to answer one of them!"

Max looked to the girl. Sam was leaning forward, her face upturned toward his, her eyes wide, her lips pulled back in a soft smile. The fire in her eyes ignited a spark in his own. He leaned forward, their faces only a foot apart. If he was playing her game, he would play his part well.

"Yes."

His voice was low, barely a whisper. She leaned closer still, and for a moment, she was silhouetted by the glow of the fireplace. He'd never felt a moment like this before. The young prince let his logic go for that moment. Maybe she was right. Maybe there *were* fairies, and magic *did* exist, and moments like this could happen all the time.

"Yes to what, Max?"

Sam's voice cut through the moment, and the magic was gone. He smiled down at her.

"Yes. I can *prove* that magic doesn't exist."

V

Max glared down at the words on the page as though they had done him a great disservice. At length, he closed the book and shoved the old tome away, his lip curling slightly. In the last month, the young prince had read every book that he could get his hands on that even hinted at the study of magic. He had combed through the stacks of the King's Library and sent riders to fetch specific texts from the

"Nothing, you just... you cut your hair, didn't you?"

She laughed, looking down at a biscuit in her hand before taking a small bite. She chewed slowly, nodding as she spoke around her food.

"Yeah, I did. I cut it about a week or so back. It was really hard to deal with all the tangles, so I just chopped it off. Much easier to manage now."

Sam nodded to the books on the table, changing the subject.

"So, nothing in your books? That doesn't prove that magic doesn't exist, Max. It just means no one has written about it."

She smiled again, one of those coy grins that he was getting used to seeing accompany the sharp twinkle in her eye. Max returned the look, his tone adopting her trademark playfulness.

"I'm not done yet. But I'm going to need your help for the next bit of my study. You see, I don't know any magic, but that doesn't mean that it doesn't exist, or that I can't actually do magic. I mean, until I prove otherwise, I must continue my research under the assumption that I am a Magician. Do you agree?"

Sam followed his trail of thought carefully, nodding as he asked the final question.

"Yes, I suppose that's the best way to go about it."

Max was unsure whether or not she was mocking him. She was smart and seemed to be following his logic, so he continued.

"Now, I have never heard of any type of magic made by any Magician. However, you have. If you can tell me how a Magician goes about making magic, I'll try it. Assuming that I am a Magician and you have your side of the facts straight, the magic will work, and you'll be proved right. If I follow your instructions, and there is no magic, then I am not a Magician, and magic doesn't exist. Agreed?"

The girl was quick as a whip. She shook her head.

"No. Even if I'm wrong, and you're not a Magician, that doesn't prove that magic doesn't exist, it only means that you can't make it."

She was right. They both knew it. After a moment, Max offered a compromise.

"Well, if I try, and fail to make magic, then will you concede that I'm not a Magician?"

Sam nodded, shoving the rest of her biscuit into her mouth, opting not to respond verbally. Max continued.

"Furthermore, if I'm not a Magician, then I don't believe that I am the best one qualified to prove the existence, or non-existence, of magic. I will withdraw from our bet, and there will be no victor. Deal?"

He stood opposite her, his back to the fireplace, the low table between them. She stayed motionless in the armchair for a few moments, letting the question hang in the air. He was trying to find a loophole, a way to justify to himself and her that he couldn't prove that magic didn't exist, but he could at least prove her wrong about one thing. Still, Max knew he had no chance of victory, only a draw or complete defeat. That is, if she went along.

Sam stood up, and the motion caused the cat by the hearth the lift his head and look up at her. The feline blinked as the girl nodded to Max.

"Agreed. But you have to do the magic properly. You can't cut corners or make mistakes. And, if at any time, I think you're not really trying, you must admit defeat and declare that magic does exist."

Max cleared his throat.

"I won't just *say* magic exists—"

She crossed her arms, snorting at his protest.

"You will if I think you're not trying hard enough!"

The boy rolled his eyes but nodded all the same.

"Alright, then. I'll try my best... but you need to help me. I need very, very specific details of magic. If I'm supposed to close my eyes and turn people to salt, then I have to know how it's done, or else I won't be able to give it a proper try. Got it?"

Sam sat back down in the armchair, her legs folding up beneath her as she settled herself.

"I've got it. What do you want to know?"

Max began his pacing, one hand scratching at his head, the other clutching his mug.

"Well, I need to know more about magic. You're my only source, as my books have failed me."

He nodded to the dozen or so tomes scattered about the table. Sam giggled.

"So, you want me to tell you fairy stories?"

Max shot her a look, his expression blank, his mind a sponge.

"Yes, exactly. Well, not just any fairy stories. I need specific ones... You said that Magicians in the stories had pets. Well, which stories? Which Magicians? Are there stories strictly about Magicians?"

Sam shook her head at that.

"No, they are never the main character. They're always either helping the hero or telling prophecies. I can't think of any stories about a specific Magician though."

Max nodded, trying to hide his inner agony. This was getting worse by the minute. He moved from the fireplace to the head of the stairs and back again.

"Well, what are some stories with Magicians in them? Not just little bits, either, but stories where magic plays a more important role."

Sam played with her hair as she thought aloud.

"Let's see, there are several. *The Bear and the Bluff* is a good one. I like *The Trembling City*, but I don't remember it so well. When I was little, I loved the one about *King Catch the Old Cat King*, but the Magician is only at the end bit."

Suddenly, it was as though a bolt of lightning had struck the girl. She sat up in the chair with a jolt, crying aloud.

"Oh! I know! *The Vanishing Princess*! It's perfect! It's got a Prince and a Princess, and they are separated by an evil Fairy Queen named Trimmil or Tremmal, I can't remember. But there is a Magician, and he plays a big part in the story!"

Max smiled politely as he imagined his pride circling a massive drain. He was about to listen to a fairy story in order to try and prove to a little girl that magic didn't exist. No, to prove he wasn't a Magician. He had no way to prove that magic didn't exist. The idea made this practice in humility all the more unbearable. Still, he would see it through. A month ago, he'd nearly killed himself out of boredom.

At least he was no longer bored. His pride could go spit in the Eastern Sea.

"Well, do you want me to tell the story?"

The young prince realized that the girl was waiting on him to start. He nodded, feigning eagerness.

"Yes. Absolutely! On with the tale!"

Sam stuck her tongue out at him and tucked a strand of hair behind her ear. She then leaned forward and, with genuine enthusiasm, launched into the story.

"Once, there was a Princess who loved a Prince, but they were forbidden to see one another. You see, the Princess had a father who was very cruel, and he didn't want her to be with the one she loved—"

Max let out an exaggerated sigh.

"I don't need the whole story, just the bit with the Magician."

Sam set her jaw, forcing her words out from behind clenched teeth.

"I'm getting to that part."

Max held up his hands in mock surrender and continued pacing. Sam waited a half a moment, as though expecting more interruptions, before picking back up where she'd left off.

"Well, the Princess' father didn't want her to be with the Prince, so he called on the evil Fairy Queen to take his daughter away to the Kingdom of the Fairies, which can only be found through magic. When the Prince heard of this, he knew that he must go rescue his True Love, but he had no allies in the Fairy Kingdom, and therefore, had no way of getting there. The Prince then went to his most trusted advisor, a Magician that the people called Old Thom and asked the wise man if he knew a way to get to the Fairy Kingdom. Old Thom did know a way. He told the Prince to fetch him three things: a large piece of honeycomb, the eyes of a turtle, and the head of a swallow. The Prince quickly gathered the items and presented them to the Magician. Old Thom took the Prince to a nearby meadow the next night. It was a full moon, and the Magician laid the materials on the ground and drew a circle about them with salt. He told the Prince that once he reached the Fairy Kingdom, he'd only have a few hours before being transported back. He told the little lord to stand in the center of the circle. The Prince was scared, but he did it anyway, so strong was his love for the Princess. The Magician clapped his hands, and the Prince was transported to the Fairy Kingdom, where he fought through the Princess' Jailers in an attempt to save his True Love. But the cell where the Princess was being kept was in the center of a maze, and though the Prince searched and fought well, he wasn't able to find her."

Max interrupted, his words goading her to hasten the story, to get back to the Magician and away from the Kingdom of Fairies.

"And? Then what?"

Sam continued, shooting Max a scornful look for his interruption.

"Well, as the Prince rounded a final bend in the maze, he spotted his love in a cell at the end of a long hallway. She called to him, and he ran to her. But even as he stretched out his arms to reach his True Love, the Prince suddenly felt himself being pulled back through the circle of salt, away from the Kingdom of Fairies and his Princess. He found himself standing alone in the middle of a meadow under the light of a full moon."

"And the Magician? Old Thom?"

Sam shook her head slowly, her voice low.

"He was nowhere to be found. And although the Prince searched the entire land, he never found the Magician, a way back to the Kingdom of Fairies, or his True Love."

As she ended the tale, there was a long silence in the upper room of the tower. Max stopped pacing and stoked the fire, adding a few logs to the top of the ones there already. He wanted it hot in the study. The cold caused him to lose focus, and he needed to concentrate on the problem. He had precious little to go on, but it was better than what his books had told him.

He turned around and asked Sam to tell the story again. She did, only this time Max interrupted every few moments to ask a question. For the most part, she was able to give a straight answer, but several times, she was of little use. She could recall the names of the Prince and Princess, but those probably didn't matter. This was an oratory tale, and he doubted he would ever find those names in a book. Other information, like the species of the swallow, Sam didn't know, and Max feared it was these smaller, seemingly insignificant facts that he would need to get right.

He had her tell him the story four times in all. Each time, he would ask more and more questions, especially concerning the Magician and, in particular, his list of materials. *Would any type of honeycomb do? What type of turtle? Why just the eyes and not the head? Were there any other markings other than the circle of salt?* After two hours and dozens of questions, he had precious little to go on, but it was good enough to start. At length, the young Prince moved to the head of the stairs and began putting on his coat.

"Alright then, I suppose I'd better go prepare."

Sam watched him, cocking an eyebrow upward. "Prepare what?"

Max smiled at her, as he buttoned up his coat.

"There's a full moon in four days. I have turtles in the laboratory, so I don't need to worry about those. Honeycomb. That's going to be tricky, since I don't know if it was for the honey or the comb, or the larvae inside. I'll need all three, so I'll have to send North for it. As for the head of a swallow, I'll have to send for that as well, as I'm sure it needs to be fresh."

Sam laughed aloud. Had she not expected this from him?

"Oh, you're sure are you? How do you know that the swallow has to be fresh?"

Max found his hat, it would be snowing around this time, and he couldn't catch a cold, as there was much work to be done.

"I figure that the swallow's head has something to do with the timing. I think it has to do with how the swallow knows where and when to migrate. Now, I don't think we need the whole head but, rather, just the brain. Still, to be safe we'll use the whole head, but I think that the brain has to be fresh, not rotten. If it's decayed, I don't think it will remember how to get back. Seems logical... in a weird way."

He headed down the stairs, the sound of Sam's giggling bouncing after him.

VI

During the next four days, Max didn't sleep more than a few hours. When he did manage to nod off, he'd wake within the hour and immediately return to his work. By the night of the full moon, the young prince had dark circles under his eyes and an odd twitch at the corner of his mouth that wouldn't go away. He stood in the laboratory, leaning heavily against the center workbench. There was a burning behind his eyes that persisted no matter how hard he blinked. He wanted, or rather *needed*, to sleep, but he couldn't. He wouldn't sleep until the experiment was done. It was the experiment that drove him. Over the past month, the idea of magic had been on his mind, but in the last four days, the quest for magic had consumed him.

The night that Sam had first told him the fairy story, he had left the tower and immediately sent out a score of riders from the King's City. Each rider rode as far as they could for a day and then visited the local villages and settlements. Specifically, the men sought stories. Max had decided that it was foolish to believe that Sam's version of *The Vanishing Princess* was the only one. As a fairy story, it was something that was handed down from one storyteller to another, which meant that, over the years, some of the details were undoubtedly muddled and mixed up. The young scholar guessed that the core elements of the story may have remained the same, but there would be many versions.

He was right. Two days before the full moon, he had nearly all of the riders' reports and, as he had expected, he had about fifty different versions of the same fairy story. He'd not been idle while the riders were away on their countryside errand. The young prince personally spoke with just about every storyteller, gypsy, traveling merchant, and nurse in the King's City, and he'd heard dozens of different versions of the tale. Putting these together with the notes from the riders, he cross-referenced all the various stories and found that there were only four things that remained consistent. It had taken him most of the day to whittle the story down to these four main points and almost as long to convince Sam that these were the core parts that really mattered. In the end, she agreed with him but only after he showed her just how different most of the stories were.

To start, many versions didn't even have a princess and, therefore, were not called *The Vanishing Princess*. Only a handful of the variations had a meadow, or even took place outside at all. In fact, most of the stories claimed that Old Thom, the Magician, had done the magic from within his tower. There were a few that said the ceremony took place in a cave, but Max discredited these, as they all came from the same scout's report, and those stories belonged to a line of people whose ancestors used to be cave dwellers. Even the Fairy Kingdom, with its Evil Queen, was only in about half of the stories. This troubled Max for a few hours, until he realized that there was no way of proving where the Magician sent the test subject, so long as the subject vanished and then returned at a later time.

In the end, it all came down to four elements. Well, five—no, six, if you wanted to be technical. The moon was always full, and there was always a Magician in the tale. The latter was of little concern to Max, as he was either a Magician, or he wasn't. He would find out very soon. And then, he would sleep.

His hollowed, tired eyes stared down at the workbench and the four materials that sat there. Directly in front of him, a small vial lay on its side, a pair of slimy eyes shining back at him through the glass. They were the eyes of an ancient snapping turtle a group of fisherman had pulled out of the river two days before. Judging by the animal's size, Max had estimated that it was anywhere from one to two hundred years old. All of the stories had included the eyes of a turtle, and enough of them used the word 'ancient' when describing the turtle for Max to believe that it was a pertinent detail. Perhaps the age of the turtle somehow symbolized the passage of time, but then again, he could be going crazy. The idea didn't frighten him anymore. He was off the charts, and he was fine with that.

The small, glass vial was dwarfed by the large, wooden crate that sat next to it. The box hummed with the vibration of a thousand honeybees, all sealed inside the crate with their entire hive. All of the stories called for bees in one form or another. Some said a single bee, some said it had to be the Queen of the Hive, but about seventy percent of the stories that Max examined stated that an entire hive was used. It was the most common material in all the different variations, and this made Max quite confident that it was correct.

Opposite the buzzing crate, there was a small, wire birdcage. Inside there was a living swallow, and it cowered under Max's sleepless gaze. The bird had been snatched far in the North nearly two days before and had been rushed via messenger bag to the

King's City. It had arrived only an hour prior, and the young prince was more proud of this component than any other. When he'd first heard Sam's version of the story, he'd suggested it was actually the brain that was needed, and it might have something to do with the fact that swallows migrate. According to his research on the story, he was right. In every story, the bird used was a migratory bird, and in about half of them, it was a swallow. Nearly a dozen of the stories said that the Magician called for the brain of a bird, not the head. A few said that a whole bird was used, but the vast majority claimed only the head was needed. One thing was made clear in all the versions. The bird had to be freshly killed.

Max took some confidence in the first three materials, but it was the fourth that was causing him the most worry. The last element of the experiment sat in a large sack at the far end of the table. Salt. In every story, a circle of salt surrounded the three other materials and whatever was being transported. In most of the tales, it was that simple. Just a circle of salt. No mention of how much salt was to be used, or how big the circle had to be. There were a few versions that said the Magician had drawn strange designs with the salt, and it was these stories that concerned Max. It was the most prominent piece of the puzzle, and it was also the most vague. Even now, with mere moments before the experiment, he was unsure of what he was going to do with the salt. He'd fiddled with some ideas, drawing out a few designs where lines of salt would encircle the individual elements and connect them to one another. He'd shown these drawings to Sam, and she said that they looked fine, but her reassurance meant little now.

"Pack light!" Master Kern ordered, "The little shits might have short legs, but we'll still have to move fast to catch 'em!"

Hart was there, her long, white hair blowing free in the breeze, drawing glances and a few murmurs from the soldiers under Kern's command. She had *requested* a temporary transfer from her command, and Master Jurgan had been hesitant to allow it. But Kern had pushed for her, and eventually, the Master of Blades had relented. Hart didn't have to say it, but she would have gone along with Second Company even without Jurgan's permission. Gwyn was her sister. And she was still missing.

"We'll be moving through the night," Kern said. "Depending on how far they've gone, we just might catch up to the wee-folk by dawn."

"But Master," a young man with a patchy beard spoke up, "some of the lads are scared of the dark. Not me, of course, but I know that Pierce and Sully still believe in ghouls."

There was a chuckle from the gathered soldiers, and the young upstart took several light blows to the arm, his comrades showing their disagreement. Kern shook his head.

"Pipe down, Pike!" he bellowed, strutting through the assembled Company, a rooster among hens. "We'll not be joking around on this one. These little folk might be the size of children, but I'll be damned if they don't kill like wild animals. So, make sure your gear is in order and your eyes are open at all times."

Another young lad called from the back of the crowd.

"So, no blinking then? Won't that make our eyes water?"

There was another wave of chuckling from the assembly, another series of playful blows. Master Kern was on the culprit like a hawk on a snake.

"Watery eyes?!" he cried, striking out with the flat of his hand, "I'll give *you* watery eyes, Gibson! This is a fighting unit! I realize that fact is lost on some of you, as we've yet to meet the enemy in pitched battle but for you veterans—I'm depending on you to keep these younger chaps in line! Last thing we need once we catch these stumpies is to have a bunch of jokesters on our hands."

A hand shot up from the middle of the pack. Kern nodded, calling on the young woman to speak.

"Yes, Miss Halsey?"

The woman's voice was blunt, almost stern.

"Just Halsey, no *Miss*," she said, bringing even more chuckles from the Company. "I'm wondering, Master, why are we going on foot? Wouldn't it make more sense to ride them down on horseback?"

There was a murmur of agreement from the soldiers, and Kern was quick to answer before any of the young upstarts could get in a snarky remark.

"A good question, Halsey!" he bellowed, making sure to project his voice for all to hear. "The answer is twofold. First, many of our horses are either still missing or severely injured. And secondly, the hills to the West are no place for a hundred idiots on horseback. One wrong move, and we're dealing with injured animals, and that will only slow us down in the long run."

"Then why is the Master of Horses going with us? She gonna make us run faster?"

"Pike!"

There was a chorus of laughter and a few harsh blows meted out by the older troops, much to the dismay of the snarky lad with the wispy beard. Master Kern nodded his approval and once again began to strut through the assembly.

"Steady now," he called in a low voice, his eyes shifting among the soldiers before giving a nod to Hart. "Master Hart is here for the same reason we all are. Well, she has more reason than most, I suppose. See lads, not only did those little bastards make us all look like fools this morning, the stumpies also captured nine of your comrades during the melee."

There was a cry of outrage and disgust from the company, and Kern joined in, fanning the flame of rage that he'd sparked.

"Yes! That's right!" he called, "They had the gall to come into our camp with their damned sticks and stones, breaking our legs and kidnapping our fellows like we were all helpless babes strolling in the woods! Now we're just supposed to let them scamper off into the sunset, back to their holes? Not on my watch, by jingo!"

Another cry, this time of agreement, rose from the assembly. Hart couldn't help but smile as she watched the scarred Master of Steel get the younglings riled up and baying for blood. With a few final words, Kern spurred them into action.

"Now, packs on! Steel sharp! It's time to hunt those little bastards down and flay them living! Second Company—Wait for it, Pike... Second Company, fall out! On the double!"

The stumpies had made small effort in hiding their trail. It was clear where they had gone: West, toward the setting sun and the foothills of the distant mountains. Moving at a quickened pace, the troops of Second Company made good time, and as darkness fell, the ground beneath their feet went from grass to rocky terrain. Master Kern was pleased with their progress and called for a brief stop. The men and women took a few moments to rest and regroup in the deep shadow of the Western mountains.

It wasn't long before the young ones began to grow restless.

"How are we gonna find them out here in the blackness?" asked Gibson.

"I reckon we'll smell 'em, Gibs," answered one of the old timers. This brought a low chorus of tired laughter from the Company.

"Not if they smell you first, Moe!" Pike's voice was raised enough for all to hear, "One whiff of your backside, and those wee-folk will take off for their hidey holes and never be seen again!"

Another chorus of chuckling, followed by a squeal from Pike as the flat of Kern's hand found him in the dark.

"Enough, lads!" the Master hissed, "this is a raiding party, not a damned day out on the lake! Keep your wits about you and your voices low!"

There was a whine from some of the new lads, but the veterans quickly put them in line with a few sharp cuffs. Another minute, they all had their breath back and were ready to go. Kern moved to the front of the pack and nudged Master Hart with his elbow. The lanky woman pulled her attention away from the rocky outcroppings around them to listen to the Commander.

"Right," Kern whispered to her, "if we keep up this pace, we could easily lose their tracks if they were to go off the main trail. I'll slow us down. You take a half-dozen and go on ahead. Keep low, stay quiet, and see if you catch any sign of them. We'll be right behind you."

Master Hart nodded and dipped back to the main group. She selected six soldiers from the front column who showed no signs of tiring and led them quickly up the trail, farther into the foothills, into the rocks and shadow.

Dawn showed itself in the East, and the troops of Second Company looked worn and pallid in the morning light. The night had not been kind, the darkness causing the bulk of the Company to lose the trail of the small folk three different times. Master Hart and her scouts were the only thing that had kept them on track. Now, the soldiers sat among the rocks of a great ravine, eating hardtack and sipping water from their canteens. A short distance up the trail, Hart and Kern debated their next move.

An old veteran with a greying top knot shook his head as he watched the two Masters argue.

"Well," he sighed, "I'd say we're lost. Not much point in going on, if you ask me. We're only getting farther from the camp and for what? Nine fools who let themselves get grabbed by a bunch of midges?"

There were one or two tired chuckles from those gathered around, but one of the young women snorted and rolled her eyes, taking a long pull from her canteen before offering a cutting retort.

"You're an angry old bastard, Marcus," she said. "If you were taken, we'd still look for you, despite the fact that you're a salty piece of meat that only cares for himself."

This drew a series of whoops and low hollers from the Company. The veteran with the top knot spat into the dust, a wry grin on his lips.

"You can call me names all day, Veera," he said. "Doesn't change the fact that you're only here searching for honor and glory, missy. Ya daft young pup! No honor in being dead. No glory in getting lost in these rocks and ravines. I'd rather be called a salty coward and be alive back at camp than get my skull smashed by some stumpy with a stick."

There were a few nods and calls of agreement from the soldiers. Veera shook her head and tousled her short hair, not ready to argue further with the respected fighter. She was Second Spear, in command of a dozen Blades, yet the old Veteran was First Spear and there was a strict chain of command. Behind her, Gibson, one of the young jokesters, spoke up.

"I'm not lost," he said, standing up and making a great show of looking around the rocky walls of the ravine, nodding to himself. "I know right where we are! This is the same spot where old Moe shat himself last night. A gopher, big as a hound, leapt out of its hole and hissed at him! Poor old fellow emptied his bowels without losing pace!"

The fighters of Second Company had a good laugh, and old Moe nodded along with the tale and swore that there was truth in it, even going as far as to point out the rock where the alleged gopher had hidden in wait for him. Only Marcus, the grizzled vet with the top knot, stayed mirthless.

"Laugh now, lads!" he called out, quieting the soldiers around, "It'll only be a matter of time before we have to sleep. Good luck getting a bit of shut-eye with a pack of midges cutting your throat!"

For a moment, there was a stunned silence in the ravine as the troops pictured the moment when they would each have to close their eyes. The fear of another attack had only just begun to grip them when a young voice called out from the crowd.

"Eat shit, Marcus!"

This brought howls of laughter from the old-timers and younglings alike. The First Spear stood, trying to see who had insulted him, but it was the Second Spear, Veera, who got the Company's attention.

"We can't do this!" the young woman cried, "We can't give in to fear and turn on each other! Our kinsmen are out there, nine of them! Maybe they aren't all from Second Company, but they are our brothers and sisters! Gearth and Trissa from the Eighth, Little Toby of the Twelfth, Master Gwyn and the smith boy, Brent!"

"Brock," corrected Gibson.

Veera nodded, a smile creeping over her face as a few chuckles rose from the soldiers seated about her.

"Aye," she continued, "Brock! The smith boy we all know so well! We can't leave them in the hands of the wee-folk!"

"Their tiny, tiny hands..." said Gibson, drawing more laughter from the crowd. Even the veteran

Marcus joined in, his short-cropped top knot dancing as he chuckled awkwardly.

"If they have to wait until we're asleep," Veera powered through the laughter, "then they truly are a bunch of cowards and weaklings! I say we don't allow our spirits to fail! We must push on!"

"She's pushing for that Master rank!" Moe called out.

"An inspiration to us all!" Gibson chimed in.

The company broke apart, still chortling good-naturedly at Veera's speech. The Second Spear made a show of spitting at their feet and cursing them for their disrespect, but her laughter spoke of her true feelings.

It was at that moment that Master Kern lay into them, his voice echoing off of the rocks around them.

"Alright, you lay-abouts!" he called out gruffly, "Look alive! The little-folk have the advantage of knowing the terrain, but we have the numbers and the discipline! Veera! What are you yammering on about? Bucking for promotion? Not till I'm in the cold, hard ground, by jingo! Harper, Moe, Greene! Get off your backsides and get up on top of that ridgeline! Gibson, one more damn word out of you, and I'll have your socks shoved down your throat, boy! Pike! Don't make me—Wait... where's Pike?"

A murmur went through the gathered Blades. No one could find the young prankster. In fact, few could remember the last time they had seen him. Within moments, Master Kern had every man and woman combing the ravine from end to end. An hour later, no one had found any sign of the young Pike. With a flurry of cursing, Kern left his Third Spear, the veteran Moe, with a half-dozen Blades to wait in the ravine just in case the straggler showed up. The rest of the Company was ordered to fall out.

They headed up the trail, farther into the mountainous terrain where the rocks grew larger, pressing in close to the path, forcing the soldiers to move in a thin line that stretched out for a quarter mile. Master Kern cursed the very stones, and Hart ordered scouts to the flanks, lest the enemy send a force to hit the middle of the line. It was one of these scouts who found the body.

They stood around, speechless. Master Hart took one look and went to the far side of the ravine, eager to be after the wee-folk. A dozen or so Blades went with her, and a few scouts were still out on patrol, but the rest of Second Company gathered about the body. Whether or not it was Pike, no one could tell. The corpse lay stretched over a rock, stomach down. The man was stripped bare from the waist up, the head removed with a series of blows from a dull blade. Odd, square runes had been carved into the flesh of his back.

Blood still drained from the wounds.

"Little *bastards!*" Kern growled.

Marcus, the veteran with the top knot, knelt close, careful not to disturb the scene.

"They broke his limbs," he said, gesturing slowly to where the man's legs and arms buckled back on themselves.

"Is it Pike?" Gibson's voice was quiet, still shocked by the scene.

The First Spear shrugged softly.

"Can't tell," he said. "Hard to recognize a face without a head."

The callousness of his words drew hisses from several of the troops gathered around. The old vet spat on the rocks.

"Hate all you want," he said. "I'm just telling what I see."

"Check his marks," Master Kern gave the order with cold contempt in his voice, and every man and woman on the hill prayed that he didn't take his anger out on them.

Marcus motioned for help and together with two others, he managed to carefully roll the body up on its side. There, on the man's right breast, was the tattooed mark of the Third Army, Second Company.

"Pikey!" Gibson's cry brought mixed reactions from the rest of the troops. Some hissed, some tried to console the young recruit, and a few spat in the dirt to ward off the ill luck of a crying warrior.

Veera spoke up, her voice once again rallying the soldiers around her.

"It might not be our friend Pike!" she called out. "Turner and Grogan were taken back at camp. Young Pike may still be alive!"

"Damn that!" Kern's voice cut each of them to their core. "This man was one of ours! Damn what his name was! His mark is ours! He was us! These filthy stains have flayed, *defiled* one of our own! This is no time to assuage fears! This is the time for vengeance."

The old fighter's eyes searched the faces of the men and women around him. There was murder in his gaze. Every member of Second Company felt his wrath and adopted it as their own. He was their avenging demon, and with him at their head, they would bring hell and death to those who had butchered one of theirs.

"I'm gonna find these little bastards!" Kern hissed. "I'll follow them into their mountains and holes, and then I'll skin them living. You came North for a crusade against evil?"

He pointed to the barbaric runes carved into the corpse at his feet.

"There it is," he said coldly. "Evil is here, and it's watching us. Eyes open, lads! Time to end this hunt. Second Company, move out!"

They followed the trail left by the wee-folk. Master Hart kept close watch on the scouts, leaving Kern to shepherd the main force. An hour after noon, and the Master of Steel called a stop. With several guards posted, Kern ordered his troops to get a few hours of shuteye. For the veterans of Second Company, it was a relief, but for the younglings, it was a chance to think back on the mutilated corpse of their comrade. Few slept, and none slept well.

The rest of the afternoon was spent crawling over rocks and ledges, climbing farther into the mountains, watching the peaks rise above them as they drew closer. The sun was just beginning to drop behind the farthest rise, when a voice called out from the back of the line. Old Moe and his half-dozen Blades were back. They had waited in the ravine as long as they dared before double-timing after the rest of the Company. The Third Spear's return was a welcome sight and even young Gibson managed a smile.

A whistle from one of Hart's foremost scouts brought a hissing order from Kern, and the column lay low in the rocks, falling silent as the Masters went to check on the front of the line. Kern returned a moment later, his voice low.

"Marcus! Veera!" he called sharply. "Up here on the double! Bring your first six Blades, ready for action! The rest of you, hold fast, but be prepared!"

The First and Second Spear each selected a half-dozen of their best fighters and followed Master Kern up the trail, away from the main column. A thousand yards further up the mountainside, there was a small shelf where the soil from above had caught and pooled. A few bushes and strangled trees had taken root, but the sparse greenery wasn't enough to hide the cleft in the rocks. Hart gestured mutely to the ground by the rocks, where the dirt was beaten down by foot traffic. Kern nodded and motioned to Marcus and Veera to stay low and encircle the entrance.

The roughly two dozen men and women of Second Company spread out and surrounded the dark opening. Each fighter found a rock, bush, or tree to hide behind, and all kept an eye on the trail that led out of the cleft in the rocks. The evening was still, only the sound of the breeze and chirp of the birds disturbed the scene.

An hour passed before there was movement.

Voices. The harsh, almost guttural grunting of the little-folk. The soldiers surrounding the cave entrance pressed themselves low into their hiding places. Seven short figures, their bodies lithe and muscled, emerged from the opening into the evening light. They carried mostly crude weapons, carved of wood and stone, except for one that held steel. The naked blade was marked with the crest of the Third Army. All of the small fighters were covered in runic tattoos, their hair and beards worn long in matted locks.

The little-folk assembled on the shelf outside the cave entrance, their words quiet, their tongue foreign. A soft whistle caused one of them to look up, briefly searching the trail leading down the mountain before returning his attention to the warrior holding the steel.

Then the soldiers struck.

Within seconds, three of the mountain men were cut down. A pair of them scampered back toward the cave entrance, only to be slain by Hart and one of her scouts who had already moved to cut off such an escape. The final two small men put up a fight, wounding several members of Second Company before being impaled by spears.

Master Hart called to her scouts and moved to secure the inside of the cave entrance with a handful of Blades. Kern moved to follow, but a cry from one of the men brought him back. The remaining attackers from the ambush stood over one of the wee-folk. The man had fallen fast, struck down by a blow to the hip. Now, he lay flat on his back, bleeding staunchly from his wounds and cursing loudly in his native tongue.

Marcus, his greying top knot askew from the fight, laughed at the small man's plight.

"Poor little midge!" he cried, "Not as easy to fight a man when he's awake, is it? Looks like ya won't be making it back to Mrs. Stumpy and the little gremlins, eh?"

"Enough, Marcus!" Veera stepped forward, but the First Spear spat in the dirt at her feet, shaking his head.

"Naw, not enough!" he said. "It's not time for one of your speeches, Veera! It's time to skin this little bastard while he's still breathing!"

There were several cries of agreement from the gathered troops. Heads turned to look at Master Kern, who stood on the edge of the ring, his face chiseled and hard as stone. The Blades wanted blood, but there was a chain of command. The old veteran said nothing, and Veera took the chance once again to defend the wounded man.

"This isn't what we came for!" the Second Spear said. "We came to find our missing comrades, not stoop to the level of the barbarous halflings! If we're to fight evil, we mustn't become evil!"

At that moment, there were several horrified cries from the cave entrance. The gathered soldiers turned, raising their steel, ready to fight. However, it wasn't the enemy that approached them from the dark maw. It was Master Hart and the scouts. The tall woman's long, white hair danced on the evening breeze as she shook her head to Kern.

"Entrance is clear," she said. "We found Pike. Gearth and Little Toby as well."

There was a groan from the younglings as Master Kern went to investigate the cave for himself. In his absence, the silence was only broken by the grunting curses of the mountain man, whose blood had begun to pool at the soldiers' feet.

A few moments later, Master Kern marched out of the cave, a fire in his eyes, a bloodied, dark shape in his hands. He stopped in the midst of the group, glaring down at the bloodied fighter, covered with runic tattoos. The Master of Steel dropped something at the man's feet.

Pike's severed head.

There was a dead pause—silence in the air as the wounded man looked from Kern, to the head, and then to the soldiers gathered over him. With another curse, the scarred warrior spat towards the bloodied head at his feet.

There was a surge of protest from the soldiers. Several called for blood. Veera tried to call for order. Marcus aimed kicks at the downed man. Master Hart moved back to the cave entrance, her mind elsewhere.

Kern's voice rose above the din, and the soldiers fell silent.

"Second Spear Veera!" he called. "Take your Spears and head back to the main column. Link up with Moe and the others. Bring them here."

The young woman cursed softly but followed her orders. The men and women of Marcus' command watched as the Second Blades left. They all knew what would happen to the stumpy once Veera was gone. The First Spear would have his way. He would peel the skin from the mountain man's flesh, and he would do it with Master Kern's blessing.

Howling screams echoed down the mountainside as the waiting soldiers of Second Company welcomed back the Second Spear and her troops. Old Moe addressed the cries openly.

"What's going on up there?" he asked. "Sounds like somebody's skinning a damned cat."

His comment drew some nervous laughter from the soldiers nearby. Young Gibson began to make a joke, but Veera's words cut him off.

"We had a scuffle with some of the mountain folk," she said. "One survived. Marcus and Kern are making an example of him."

The youngsters were quiet, but the Third Spear, old Moe, wasn't so easily shaken. He'd been on several campaigns and had seen the horror and the boredom of war.

"Skinning a stumpy, eh?" he said casually. "Won't make for much of a pelt. Leave it to Marcus to waste the effort."

Veera spat into the dirt, openly disgusted.

"Kern wants the Company up the hill," she said, raising her voice above the chuckles brought on by Moe's comments.

The old Third Spear nodded, rising to his feet and waving to the Blades down the line. His voice was calm, years of service showing in his zen-like approach to the circumstances.

"Might as well stretch our legs, lads!" he called, the troops around him following his lead—rising to their feet and stretching. "Eyes open, steel at the ready. Never know when those little bastards will turn up for more."

As the column headed up the mountainside, the screams from above faded away. Veera spat into the dirt, waiting until the rest of the soldiers had moved on before ordering her Blades to follow.

That night, Second Company made camp on the shelf outside of the cave entrance. A picket line was placed, with watchmen keeping an open eye on the mountainside around them. While most of the men and women slept soundly outside, Master Hart and several of the scouts pressed deeper into the cave, wary of any mountain folk that might try to attack from the depth of the darkness.

Master Kern made his way past the cleft in the rock face. Stepping over the bundled bodies of Gearth and Little Toby and the pool of blood where he'd found Pike's head, he moved along the path, following the cool air downward until he found the spot where Hart had set up for the night.

The Master of Horses greeted him with a low grunt, her eyes gazing into the blackness below. The Master of Steel settled down on the rocks next to Hart, letting a long sigh out into the darkness.

"So, they're down there, eh?" he asked.

"That's my best guess," Hart said.

The two sat in silence, both contemplating the darkness of the tunnels for several minutes. Kern rubbed at his hands, massaging dried blood from the crags in his skin. He'd ordered the body of the small folk disposed of, but Marcus insisted on putting the mountain man's skin on a pole outside the cave entrance. Kern allowed it. The younglings needed to understand that they were in it now. No turning back.

"You think they're alive?" he asked quietly. Kern hadn't dared ask the question, but now, facing the darkness, he pushed to test his peer's resolve.

Hart was, as always, unreadable.

"Could be," she said. "Don't know why the wee-folk would bother bringing them all the way up the mountain if they were only going to slit every one of their throats. Doesn't make any sense."

"Barbarians," Kern muttered, as though the word explained such actions. "They killed Pike and those two from the Eighth. Why wouldn't they butcher the rest?"

"Pike's body was a message," Hart said blankly. "Maybe we didn't understand what that message said, but it's plain to me that they didn't expect us to follow them this far."

"And Gearth? Little Toby?" he asked. "What were they?"

The Master of Horses stared into the dark, her voice low, thoughtful.

"To you and I? They were friends, comrades," she said. "To the wee-folk? They were soldiers. I doubt they had any use for enemy soldiers."

"What are you on about?" Kern asked, suspicious that the long-haired woman was finally addressing what had been on her mind since they had left the great camp the day before.

"Well," Master Hart continued, "Their main force hit us from the North, but Gwyn was on the East side of the camp, by the horses. And the smith boy, Brock. He was on the South side, by the great fire. I think the mountain folk were watching us for some time. They hit us hard and cut our horse lines, not to hurt us but to distract from their real purpose."

"And what was that?" Kern asked.

"I think they were after knowledge," she said. "They are armed with little more than sticks and stone clubs. They have no steel. None of their own, anyway. So, they take a smith. They ran across the plains to fight us. They have no horses. They take Gwyn."

The Master of Steel smirked, spitting down into the darkness and shaking his head.

"I think you're giving these stumpies far too much credit," he chided. "They are savages, barbarians. You saw Pike's body. That's what they are, Hart. Nothing more."

"I saw what you all did to that wounded man," she retorted bluntly. "Perhaps we're all savages. Maybe some of us just have better weapons and march in straight lines."

There was quiet in the tunnel for a moment. At length, the old Master sighed heavily as he stood up.

"Maybe you're right," he said. "In any case, we'll not be following them into that blackness. We've no idea what's down there. I'll not have a hundred men die for the sake of a half-dozen. Get some sleep, Hart. We head out at first light."

The Master of Steel moved back up the tunnel, checking on those camped inside the entrance before heading out to make sure the perimeter was secure. After taking stock of the makeshift camp, he bedded down by the fire. He stared up at the shadowy image of the bloodied pole, the skin of the mountain man still clinging to the wood. He drifted off to a light sleep, listening to the sound of the men chuckling at one of Gibson's jokes.

The early morning light was met with the ring of steel and the cries of startled men. Those on watch, the Fifth Spear and her Blades, were caught off guard as a wave of mountain folk struck from above and below. By the time those near the cave entrance were awake enough to understand what was happening, the guards had been overrun, and the small-folk were on them. Marcus, the First Spear, screamed wildly as he cut down a pair of fiends that tried to rush him with stone-tipped weapons. Veera moved her Blades back from the edge of the shelf, forming a tight group to cover the medics who pulled the wounded toward the cave entrance. Old Moe stood over Gibson. The boy was screaming, his leg shattered by stone hammers. The old Third Spear fell with a crude, wooden javelin in his gut, and the young lad's screams were soon cut short by another hammer blow.

Master Kern shouted above the melee, a cut on his face bleeding into his open mouth.

"Back!" he yelled. "Into the cave! We'll hold them at the entrance!"

The soldiers of Second Company moved backwards, stepping over the bodies of friends and enemies alike on their way to the relative shelter of the cleft in the rocks. Veera, Second Spear, already held the entrance and allowed the rest of the soldiers to pass by, hacking a limb from a howling mountain man who charged Marcus' open back.

Once the soldiers were inside, the wee-folk stopped pressing the attack. They were smart enough to know better than to rush the bottle-neck of the cave entrance. Instead, they pranced about the shelf outside, hacking at the bodies and smashing the bones of the wounded. Moments after the attack had begun, the mountainside shelf where the soldiers had slept was awash with blood and broken bodies.

Inside the cave, the men and women of Second Company caught their breath and hastily tended to their wounds. The wounded soldiers that Veera's Blades had managed to pull inside were now strewn about the floor, their moans echoing off of the tight space created by the rocks. The clamor and confusion of those still upright mixed with the cries of the wounded to create an unholy din in the confines of the cave.

"Quiet!" Master Kern bellowed.

The voices and cries of the soldiers went nearly silent, only a few unconscious groans from the floor and some panting from those still on their feet could be heard. The Master of Steel cursed and fought past the crowd of soldiers toward the light of the entrance. He peered out past the row of shields and spears blocking the path inside.

"Bastards!" he muttered, watching the small mountain warriors on the shelf as they slashed and hacked at the bodies of the dead and dying soldiers of Second Company.

At his elbow, Marcus, urged the commander to fight.

"We can rally," he said hotly. "A shield wall bristling with steel would push them off that shelf and down the mountainside beyond! We should go out now, Master!"

Kern shook his head, his eyes searching the trees outside the clearing.

"No," he said, "there's no telling how many of them are out there. Maybe they are waiting just beyond our line of sight with two hundred more fighters. We've underestimated them enough. I'll not do it again. We hold here. Master Hart!"

The Master of Horses appeared beside Kern without a word, her long, white hair wild from the fighting. The Master of Steel spat in the direction of the wee-folk outside the cave entrance before turning to face the woman.

"Take your scouts, find me a way out of this damn cave. I'll not die in a dirty, dark hole. Go. Now."

Hart nodded and took her leave, a handful of Blades peeling away from the surrounding soldiers to follow as she moved into the unknown depths of the tunnels. The Master and her scouts had only been gone a short while when Marcus spotted activity near the edge of the shelf.

The surly First Spear called out, and Master Kern joined him to watch as the barbaric mountain folk tore an evergreen tree up from the rocky ground, scrawny roots and all. By the time the men in the cave knew what was happening, a horde of the small fighters materialized from the mountainside and were rushing the entrance, the uprooted tree held before them like a battering ram.

Kern was confident. The wee-folk had numbers, but his Blades had shields, armor, and training.

"Hold fast!" he called, the soldiers about him bracing for the impact of the charge. "Shields!"

The armor of Second Company held firm as the angry flesh of the mountain people smashed against the shield wall. The evergreen tree, little more than an overgrown bush, made for a horrible ram, its wispy point bending away from the Blades and smashing into the cave ceiling over their heads.

Marcus gave a callous laugh as he chopped down a wriggling foe.

"Stupid midges!" he cried, "Never rushed a shield wall before, eh?"

The Blades around the First Spear joined in the gloating and, for a brief moment, the fight was going well.

Then, there was a panicked screech from the base of the tree, still lodged near the cave's entrance. Flames licked the evergreen, eating away at the dried bark but refusing to light the living sap. Thick, white smoke filled the cave. Moments later, the Blades of Second Company were coughing and choking, their eyes streaming with tears as they flailed wildly against their foes.

The wee-folk renewed their attack, with fresh fighters rushing toward the cave from the shelf. They used their stone tipped weapons and bare arms to keep the soldiers inside the crevice, many of their numbers falling as the Blades within struck out blindly. Moments later, the men and women in the cave had lost the fight, overcome by the smoke that filled their eyes and lungs.

The mountain fighters removed the smoldering tree husk and set about clearing the armor-clad warriors of Second Company from the cave. The wounded were killed, murdered where they lay on the stone floor. The darkness of the rocks became a bloody pit of hellish smells and cries as the wee-folk went to work on the corpses with their stone knives.

Only a dozen Blades remained alive. They were dragged outside to the shelf, stripped of their armor, their belts used to bind their hands. The throng of wild warriors collected all the weapons and shields they could, bundling them in the cloaks of dead soldiers as they prepared to travel.

The dirty horde set off at a quick pace, ten warriors to each prisoner, a half-dozen more following behind with the bundles of looted weapons. They went through the cave, over the broken bodies of Second Company, through pools of blood and grime and into the darkness beyond.

Down, down into the dark the horrible band moved, their feet pounding out a muffled, broken cadence on the worn stone. The air grew cold and damp, moisture causing the walls of the tunnels to glisten softly in the flames of their torches. The path grew narrow, and more than once the prisoners had to be led single-file through tight areas where the rock walls caused a bottleneck. The wee-folk navigated the tunnels with speed and practiced ease, pushing quickly on, down into the darkness, their prisoners in tow.

After a great while, the cramped pathways opened up into a series of underground caverns. The cool air was stifled by smoke from a hundred smoldering dung fires, their light a muted glow in the low spaces. Small, pale figures crawled forth from dirt burrows, clawing at the prisoners with scarred hands, calling out for flesh with swollen tongues.

Two of the dazed members of Second Company were given over to the mob. The naked horde of cave denizens descended on the prisoners. The pair cried out in the red darkness as a hundred hands tore them apart, their blood seeping into the stained ground of the cave floor as the masses began to feed. The remaining soldiers of Second Company awoke to the horror and struggled against their bonds. First Spear Marcus kicked out at his captures and cursed them.

"You feckless worms!" he spat. "Bastard midges! Give me a blade! I'll butcher you like the animals you are!"

His insults were drowned out as the wee-folk dragged him and the remaining soldiers past the carnage of the feast, into the great open chamber beyond. A wide trough was set with fire, and by the light of it, the prisoners beheld a large stone table at the center of the cave. The wee-folk seized hold of Marcus, his screams the loudest, and brought him forward. They pulled his limbs wide and stretched him across the table on his back.

As the First Spear cursed and spat at the figures holding him, the rest of the prisoners were herded into a series of pens in a dark corner of the cave, their feet hobbled and hands bound tight. There were others there already. A man and a woman, both branded with the mark of the Third Army. One had long, white hair.

Marcus' screams turned to hoarse, ragged breaths as two of the wee-folk began to slowly stack large, flat stones on his chest. His struggling ceased as his muscles seized up.

"Bastards..." he managed to wheeze before the pressure on his ribs became too great. Eventually, as the number of stones grew, there was a cracking and the man's breathing became choked, his lungs punctured.

The fire in the trench burned low as the wee-folk removed the stones and slathered the First Spear's broken body in clay and mud. With words of drooling satisfaction, they rolled the encrusted meat onto the coals to cook.

It was then that the scouts struck.

The surrounding mountain men were caught unaware as the ten or so Blades under Master Hart materialized from the shadows and struck into the guards by the trench. The attackers slaughtered nearly a dozen of the fighters before the wee-folk understood what was happening and scattered into the various tunnels that ran off of the chamber.

Master Hart moved into the pens, pushing aside the soldiers until she came upon the two that had been there since before Second Company's capture. She pulled the crumpled woman with the long, white hair upright. Hart embraced her sister briefly.

Turning, the Master of Horses barked orders to the men around her. The prisoners were cut loose and armed with what weapons could be spared. Hart held Gwynn upright and pointed to the darkest tunnel on the far side of the cavern. The remnants of Second Company darted toward the hole without hesitation, too shocked by the blood and stench of the wee-folk's domain to think.

Across the cave, the cannibals gathered together by the fiery trench where Marcus' body burned. With barking, guttural cries, they surged forward, a horde of mud, teeth, and claws. Two of the scouts held the entrance to the dark tunnel, their bloodied steel flashing in the red light of the fires. Hart and Gwynn led the rest of the Blades onward, deeper into the earth and dark, the sounds of fighting dying away behind them as the pair of soldiers from Second Company held for as long as they were able before succumbing to the horde.

In the darkness of the tunnels, many of the Blades lost their way, stumbling into the dirt and crying out for their comrades until they died alone or were discovered by the wee-folk. The core group of soldiers, led by the sisters, hurtled through the dark tunnels, always forward, always downward, the howls and snarls of cannibals chasing them from one corner to the next.

Water trickled along the tunnel at their feet, clear and free. Gwynn's cracked voice called to those around her—if water could escape, so could they.

Hope was brief, turning to horror as the survivors discovered that the path disappeared into a black, endless void as the water poured over an underground ledge, falling into the darkness beneath them. The small group paused in the darkness, catching their breath, contemplating their next move.

The red light of the cannibal's torches glowed on the rocks around them—there were screeches and the clash of steel in the close quarters of the tunnel. Two of the soldiers fell instantly, their bodies slowing the tide of the horde for a few precious moments. Hart shoved her spear into the face of the enemy as the man on her right side died screaming. Veera, the Second Spear and last surviving member of Second Company, threw herself headlong into the fray, swinging a broken spear haft at the twisting mass of cannibals.

"Go!" she screamed, her body jerking awkwardly as the fiends got hold of her and began to sink their teeth in.

There was a lull in the fighting as the beasts tore the fresh corpse apart. Hart grabbed Gwynn's arm and pulled her to the ledge. They stared down into the blackness, the cold water falling away from them and out of sight. Behind them, the horde snarled and began once more to surge forward, their teeth and claws warm and red from the flesh of the fallen.

The sisters leapt into the abyss, cold air rushing past—their long, white hair streaming out behind them as they plunged into nothingness.

The black lake rippled softly, lapping at the sandy edge of the shore. The air in the cavern was sweltering, drafts of heat wafting up from the tunnels carved in the great walls. A warm, deep glow pulsed life into the cave, illuminating the surface of the lake as two figures staggered through the shallows, each helping the other to stay upright. They collapsed on the sandy shore at the foot of a massive pillar, an ancient monolith carved with great, square runes. Hart stared up at the marker, her sister's hand clasped in hers.

This was how the daughters of man first found their way to Dennwaith, the Ancient Realm of the Dwarves.

THE NAME OF FEAR

Stepping off of the boat and onto the dock, the old man took a deep breath. Though the sky was grey and overcast, the breeze was crisp and cool. It was a welcome change from the stodgy, often rancid air of the city. He looked up the pier toward the cluster of buildings at the island's center. The old buildings were worn, nearly crumbling, a fair match for the castle beyond.

He waved to the boatman and headed inland, carefully skirting the puddles and gutters that littered the dockyard. By the time he reached the city center, the mud was unavoidable, his shoes caked with the muck and manure of the streets. The old man shook his bald head and muttered softly to himself, his white beard becoming untucked from his traveling cloak.

It was dark by the time he passed through the island city, finally reaching the gates of the ruined castle shortly after the seventh bell. From the darkened guardhouse over the gate there came a gruff call.

"Halt!" it cried, sharp and sudden. "*Who comes creeping up from sewers to walk with nobles? Speak and be recognized!*"

The traveler stood still and allowed a smile to spread across his face. Though he had never been to the castle, he knew the words spoken and felt immediately at home. He called back toward the hidden voice.

"*Nobles? I see no Nobles here! Only the demons of the damned and the depraved!*" he recited the words verbatim before adding his own. "I have come on the command of the Lord of the Keep, my friend! I have his summons on my person."

There was a scuffle from the dark room overhead and the hissing strike of a match as a lantern was lit. A grimy face with a slender nose peered down at the traveler.

"You must be a Reader!" it crooned, "to know the words of Gill when spoken! I'll be right down!"

The old man gave a nod and a small smile as the face, still lit by the lamp, disappeared from the high window of the guardhouse. He was a Reader, and he had studied every book in the Great Libraries for many years. It wasn't often he met someone who quoted verse at him, and when it did happen, it was rare to hear it spoken with such confidence as the gatekeeper. There was a grating of rusty metal, and the thick, dark gate swung inward.

"*Enter, then, my mortal friend!*" the man, no longer towering over the road from his window, stood small and hunched before the old Reader. "*But be wary of the tongues of the Nobles, as they are quick as serpents!"*

The old man continued to smile as he reached inside his cloak and withdrew the letter, which bore the Lord's seal. The crooked little fellow was butchering the written word now, perhaps in a vain attempt to impress the learned man treading on his patch of muddy road. The thought sprang into the traveler's mind that some people would be better off saying less and listening more, a common thought in his line of work.

"Here is my summons, good fellow" he said, handing the crisp paper over to the grimy man.

The gatekeeper had a shine of interest in his eye—not for the summons, which he dismissed after a quick glance, but toward the old man standing tall before him. He returned the paper with a nod and a smile.

"Gill is an old favorite," he crooned. "Though, I've never agreed with his writings concerning the tree-folk. Bit of a looney way to look at things, thinking men can just become trees as long as they act like them."

The Reader's smile was strained, a twinge of distaste pulling at his guts. The little man was reaching too far now, and he was out of his depth.

"Am I expected then?" he asked in an attempt to guide the conversation. "Or has the Lord of the Island forgotten about me?"

The gatekeeper shook his head, tearing his gaze away from the Reader and gesturing up the cobbled lane with disinterest.

"Naw," he muttered, "you're expected. Every day, the little lord trots down here and asks whether you've been spotted. Sometimes twice."

The hunched fellow turned back, his nose catching the light of the lantern as he gave a whistling snort.

"Not sure what he wants you for," he continued, still blocking the Reader's path with his hunched body. "He didn't give two shits about the written word before sending for you. Not much of a thinker, that one. Spends too much time with his games, not enough time stretching the only muscle that matters."

Here, the twisted little man tapped the side of his head with his free hand. The Reader cringed inwardly and abandoned his faux smile all together.

"I'd best not keep him waiting, then," the old man said, shifting his weight and making to move through the gate.

The gatekeeper remained planted on the muddy cobbles just inside the doorway, his mind bent on conversation.

"I think the world would be a better place if more people read the books," he stated. "Why have you all gotta keep them locked away in the libraries? Who made the rule that only the privileged should have access, eh?"

The Reader's patience had reached its end. The doorkeeper, a simpleton, would not keep him from his purpose any longer. He drew himself up until he nearly towered over the crooked man.

"The King's Edict of 878," he said, moving forward, forcing the gatekeeper to step aside. "After the Pauper's Rebellion, the Monarchy forbid the distribution of literature to the lower class. A learned man would know this."

The guard stood aghast, his breath whistling through his slender nostrils. The Reader moved away, his mud-caked boots thudding a satisfactory cadence as he mounted the cobbles and headed toward the keep in the distance. As a final flourish against the man's supposed intellect, he called back over his shoulder.

"And Gill didn't write anything about tree-folk," he said. "That was Fulfneer. Gill advocated for the reallocation of property away from the working class. Leave the word to the learned and mind your gate, friend."

The muttered curses of the scorned gatekeeper followed the Reader only a short way up the street. The evening brought a chill to the island air, which no doubt drove the twisted little man inside with the rest of the local slack-jaws. The bearded old man took no joy in correcting the fellow's ignorance. He would rather have a decent conversation with a peer than constantly be forced to remind both others and himself that he was more learned than most. Every so often, he would get a snippet of discussion that was mildly interesting, but it rarely took him long to discern the source of another's knowledge. He was almost certain that the gatekeeper had perused a copy of *Thirteen Important Tales*, a leaflet leftover from the last rebellion. The words of the text were not deemed dangerous enough by the Monarchy to warrant complete eradication, but they did serve to embolden some members of the local populace to airs of grandeur. Authors like Gill, Heppert, Meinhenn, and

Trollsteig were all worthy of praise, but they did little to stir sedition among the populous.

The Reader arrived at the door of the crumbling keep and was again hailed by a hidden guard. Again, he showed his paper with the Lord's seal, and again, he was allowed to pass, this time without unnecessary conversation.

In the hall beyond, he found the Lord of the Keep. A small, squat man with greying hair and a furrowed brow, the lord sat near the hall's great fire, inspecting a wooden board that was set with carved game pieces.

The greying man raised his head as the Reader approached.

"Took your time getting here," he said, obviously vexed.

The Reader didn't waste time with a smile, seeing that the lord wasn't a man to suffer pleasantries. He spoke plainly.

"Your summons said that you had need of a Reader," the visitor said. "I am the sure you will find my skills wo—"

The squat man by the fire waved him off and returned his attention to the game board before him, adopting a tone of annoyance rather than anger.

"Don't weigh my mind with your accolades, priest," he said. "As long as you can read, I don't care."

The Reader's eye twitched, his jaw tightening. He'd long suffered the ignorance of lesser men, fools thinking themselves worthy of status. This fat little lord was no different. He cleared his throat gently.

"I'm not a priest, my Lord," he said calmly. "My name is Milton , I'm—"

The little man gave a snorting chuckle.

"I said that I didn't care," he interrupted, "And I meant it. I truly don't care who or what you are, as long as you keep the boy occupied. Don't let his words and trickery get to you. He's already chased off every teacher on the island and every tutor willing to make the journey from the mainland. His standard studies are complete anyway, all I need is for his mind to remain engaged until I decided what to do with him."

The lord shifted a carved piece on the table and then swiveled the board around to view the game from the opposite angle. Milton watched in silence, slightly unsure how to respond. He'd guessed that his presence had been requested, not for the lord, but for a younger student, as most of his tasks involved reciting the words to eager young minds. Oddly enough, he wasn't aware that the lord had a boy. In fact, the Great Library had no children on record as living in the castle at all. He guessed that the squat little lord had no idea that such records even existed.

When the Reader failed to move, the little man looked up briefly and pointed to a staircase at the far end of the hall.

"Top floor, West tower," he said with a sigh. "He'll be awake. No doubt he'll be up all night, and you two can talk until you run out of words."

Milton wasted no more time on the fat little man. The Reader left the lord with his mind wrapped around the board game, his eyes boring into the pieces as though willing them to move on their own. Exiting the hall, the old man felt the draft of the night air as he ascended the stairs and headed to the West tower. By the time he reached the top floor, his pace had slowed, in part due to his shortness of breath, part due to the almost criminal lack of light.

Not a single flame lit the stones of the corridor outside the far rooms of the West tower. The old man stood still and allowed his eyes to grow accustomed to the faint illumination of the moon as it splashed in through a high window at the end of the hallway. Moving slowly, he made his way to the last door, his brow furrowed, vexed at the lack of consideration the Lord of the Keep showed for his son, or better yet, his learned guests.

He raised a hand and gave the door a sharp, resounding knock. A voice from the other side, small but steady, answered.

"Enter! Make haste and leave the darkness behind!"

Reader Milton smiled in the corridor. The boy was quoting Hessen, a rare treat to hear from the mouths of the common folk outside of the Libraries. The ancient author was one of the first to leave behind the written word, and most of his poems lingered on the edge of prophetic—high-minded matter for a child.

The aging man opened the door and stepped over the threshold into a stunningly lit room. He turned to close the door and saw the grim hallway behind briefly awash with a fiery glow. For a last, split second, he wondered once again why the path to the boy's chamber was kept so dark on such a cold night. But then he turned back to the room and stood in awe of what seemed to be a thousand candles, wicks trimmed and burning merrily. From great, poured pillars, to tall, dipped sticks, there didn't seem to be an open spot on floor and walls of the chamber.

Virtually every visible space was occupied by some form of slowly melting wax.

The boy stood with his back to the door, a long-stemmed match in one hand, a glass of water in the other.

Closing the door, Milton focused again on the boy, as he finished his water, set the glass on a low table and moved to sit. The lad had a thin, pale face and dark, almost hollow eyes. He looked like a ghostly waif, yet moved with the grace and confidence of a bird on the wind. The old man straightened his cloak and brushed his beard with a quick gesture, remembering suddenly that he represented the Great Libraries, as well as himself. The lad had quoted Hessen, perhaps he knew more of the ancient authors.

"I come from across dark tide," he said, trying to avoid the natural cadence that often accompanied the old words. *"Though some would say I seek to hide, welcome me and I will confide, all that I know will be yours."*

The boy's sunken eyes lit up as bright as the candles about them, a smile on his lips, teeth straight and clean. Apparently, he knew more than just Hessan and understood the words to not be the Reader's. The lad pushed a chair out from the table, rising politely as he motioned for his guest to sit.

"Rest," the lad's voice was calm, and Milton listened close to each word, *"Rest of bone, Rest of Flesh. Eat of Meat, Drink of Mead. Rest to Man, Rest to Steed. Fight Tomorrow, Strong Arm will need."*

The Reader leaned back in the chair, his mind whirling. The boy knew old scripture. Very old. Though he had recognized the words, Milton was unsure who had written them. Not because he was unlearned, but because no one at the Great Libraries was sure of the author. Some said it was a shaman from the West, others claimed that a teacher from beyond the North Sea had spoken the words after setting foot on dry land. The fact that this young lad knew the words at all was astonishing to the old Reader.

He wanted to question the little lord before him and find out how he had come by such ancient knowledge. Yet, something told him to wait. The lad obviously didn't leave the tower often. Perhaps he rarely had opportunity to speak the words. Perhaps if the old Reader placated him for a while, the lad would open up and, perhaps, tell him how he knew such things.

Milton thought back to his time in the restricted sections of the shelves of the ninth floor of the North tower of the Great Libraries. He had spent many weeks of his younger years pouring over the various manuscripts stored there. He flipped through the pages of his memory until he found something suitable for the young master before him. The words were old, a shepherd by the name of Joana had first penned them in the time of the Sundering.

"*To follow,*" Milton said, his eyes closed as he read the page from his memory, "*To graze on the grass of the master. Man is but a sheep, seeking out greener pastures. But who is man's shepherd? Who is the student, and who is the teacher? Is this a question of who or what? That is the answer I'm after.*"

The page in his mind's eye grew blurry and faded away from sight. That was all his memory could recall.

When Milton finished and opened his eyes, he saw that the boy also had his eyes closed. There was a small smile on the lad's face. The Reader had a feeling that Joana the Shepherd's words were already known to him.

The boy's eyes remained closed as his voice recited more verse.

"*And when the question is answered,*" he said, "*I will follow the master. I will follow into darkness that voice which calls me. For though I am the shepherd, I am the student, seeking the words of the wise, the learned. Give me lessons, give me knowledge, and I will eat my fill of both darkness and light. I am the shadow, both darkness and light.*"

Even as the little lord spoke, Reader Milton could see the words revealed on that blurry page in his mind. The boy spoke the Shepherd's words, more clear than those who had studied the restricted scripts.

The old man's eyes narrowed. He was tired of these games. The boy was dabbling in knowledge that he couldn't possibly understand. Few men did. He opened his mouth to speak, perhaps ask the lad where he had read such verse, but before he could speak a word, the little lord opened his eyes and smiled.

"Where are you from?" he asked softly. "How was your journey to this land of the seafolk?"

Milton nearly answered in his own voice, but something in the lad's tone made him pause. It was a half moment before he was able to see past the seemingly casual question. It was the term, *land of the seafolk*. No laymen used words like that, not outside of the Great Libraries. It was possible that the boy was only injecting something that he'd read into his everyday language, but something about the lad made the Reader doubt it.

The boy was still playing games. No, more than that. He was testing the old man, just as the Reader had tested him. And Milton had almost fallen for the trap. He was lucky. It was his guess that the boy would never talk to him with his own words. Not until the lad respected him enough. To gain the lad's respect, Milton decided that he would need to show the little lord his own. Perhaps respecting the boy as a peer would allow Milton a look inside his mind.

He decided to play along. The boy spoke of the seafolk, in the words of the seer called Omer. He would answer in the words of Omer's protégé, Gretal.

"The sea," he began, "the sea is home to all sorts. Men would think nothing beyond fish or mighty serpents, but lords have built their houses upon the sea, and therefore, men are also creatures of the sea. To enter the home of seafolk, that is to enter into the grace of one enlightened. But if the seafolk mean men harm, then it is best to beware, or better yet, stay on land, dry and dumb."

The boy nodded slowly, and the look in his eye told Milton that he'd made the right choice in continuing to use the words of the ancient scholars.

The little lord leaned forward, his voice bowing low as his eyes searched the Reader's face.

"Would you tell me if you knew? Would you whisper the name of the darkness?" The hairs on Milton's neck stood up as he recognized the words—Chaise, the mad king of long nights. The lad spoke with such reverence, the old man half expected to find one of the author's lost tomes hidden under the lad's mattress.

"*I ask not for me, but for the hope that one day the darkness will not ask my name, on that day, I will sleep and dream of nights spent in solace. But the day brings the light, and the light knows my name and calls to me often. No more is my name my own. Sleep is no more, solace is no more.*"

The words of Chaise were full of dread and despair, and the old Reader wondered how a young man could speak them with such devotion. There was a look of hopelessness in the little lord's eyes, and Milton couldn't help but respond with words of hope and kindness.

"*Be brave, my ward,*" he spoke gently, the tender words of Sister Rhanha pouring from his lips with practiced ease. "*For there is never a fear so great that it cannot be overwhelmed with love. There is only one great fear, and it is not known. But love has many faces. All are known to you, even now in the midst of your fear. What great fear can overpower such love? None.*"

The little lord sat back, his eyes misting over as the Reader finished Sister Rhanha's passage. Milton thought that perhaps the boy was touched in the head. Were he the son of a fisherman, he would run screaming into the sea, but as the son of a lord, he was merely imprisoned in his tower, cursed to his loneliness, a harm only to himself.

Milton decided then to speak to the boy's father. He would implore the man to send the boy to the Great Libraries. He could be the source of much study by th—

"I know the name of fear," the boy said, his voice low, slightly trembling. "I have stared into the darkness and into the sun the same. Both have filled me with horror, but only the darkness has stared back. Fear is not for the weak, but for the strong. I must be strong indeed, for I have been subject to the greatest of fear. The darkness has spoken to me, and it has called my name."

The old Reader's eyes narrowed as he searched the boy's face. He didn't know the words, not from the books in the Great Libraries or his own research, but he felt that they were heavy with import and woven with truth. Could they be the lad's? If they were indeed the little lord's own words, there was only one response.

He dared answer the unfamiliar words with his own.

"And what then," he asked, "is the name of fear?"

The little lord looked up at him and shook his head sadly.

"I cannot tell you the name," he said. "Only you can hear the name, spoken from the mouth of such fear. You must see the face of fear, Reader. Do wish to see that face, the one that visits here and whispers to me of great knowledge?"

Reader Milton nodded mutely, his mouth unable to find his own words to answer. The boy nodded in return and solemnly stood and began to snuff out the surrounding flames.

Patches of shadow crept into the room as the boy moved, slowly but steadily, from candle to candle. The air around them was suddenly thick and stale. The Reader pulled at his collar and gasped softly for breath. He thought he could hear his heart pounding in his chest, but as the boy continued to smother the flames, he realized that the sound was from the walls of the tower itself. The room became as a drum, the walls resounding with a pounding rhythm as the darkness grew stronger, drowning the light with a crushing wave of black. Milton could barely breathe. His head split with a piercing pain as the stones around him cried out, their edges grinding against one another as the blackness filled the room to bursting.

As the last light was extinguished, there was a sudden crack in the ceiling. The Reader whirled round to look and there, in the darkness above, the sky was exposed before him. A black maw spewed forth and devoured the room, churning and boiling with heavy malice. The old man tried to find his voice, but his tongue was useless. Only the little lord was able to speak, and the only word he spoke was the name of that great fear that now consumed the Reader's mind, body, and soul.

TRUE BELIEVER

I

The boatman was fat, and his sweat reeked of alcohol. His eyes closed as he dabbed his face with the edge of the worn, greying towel he kept draped over his left shoulder. The sun beat down on the city harbor, and it was with a grunt that the fat man leaned over the tiller and spat a lazy slop of brown juice into the river. With a sigh, the boatman wiped his stained chin and watched a pair of sturdy men in worn traveling cloaks move down the dock toward him. The pair moved with purpose.

The two hooded travelers set their packs in the bottom of the vessel and helped push away from the busy dock. After a few minutes, the single sail was snapping at a stiff breeze, pulling them against the river's gentle current. They passed the fishing market and then the cattle yards. After a quarter hour, the noise of the settlement was dying away, and the river could be heard thumping against the bow. The young, broad-shouldered man sat in the belly of the boat, his back to the mast and his eyes closed, as if in contrition. The grey-haired man settled closer to the bow, his dark eyes scanning the horizon ahead.

It was only after they had rounded the bend of the river West of town and unfurled the sail that the boatman attempted a conversation. The younger of the two remained faithful to his silence. The elder of the pair answered questions, yet never met the boatman's eye. His attention was ever forward, up the river.

"How far upriver are you wanting to go? The message wasn't very specific."

The old man kept his words short.

"As far as we must."

They passed a group of small children, up to their ankles in the muck along the bank of the river. One little lad carried a short frog-spear, another waved at the boatman. The fat man smiled and nodded back. His attention returned to the men in his boat. His eye fell to the blade in its sheath—the large hilt cradled in the older man's arms.

"I see you've got steel with you. You're part of the militia, then?"

"Our steel is not of the militia. Our Lord has given us great purpose. We bring the Light."

The boatman leaned over the tiller and spat over the side, scanning the far bank with a twinkle in his eye and a smirk pulling at his lips.

"Your Lord... Does he pay well?"

The Holy Man stiffened.

"You'll receive your coin, boatman."

"Houst."

"Excuse me?"

"My name's Houst. I'll not have you calling me *boatman* for the entire trip."

He leaned back and studied the sky above the small, flat-bottomed boat for a moment before adjusting his grip on the tiller to dab sweat from his eyes with his greying towel. He squinted against the sunlight.

"As long as the weather holds, we'll continue upriver at a steady pace. But if we lose this wind, we'll have to pull our way up. Now, I don't care if you pay like there's ten of you—I only see two. That's not enough to fight the current when the breeze stops."

The Holy Man glanced at the broad-shouldered young man before turning to look back upriver.

"I bring the Holy Fire. We'll be fine."

Houst looked from the old man to the lad still sitting with his back to the mast. He raised an eyebrow and leaned back, his foot propped up on the seat in front of him.

"I've heard of your lot. White Scarfs. Zealots on a quest, fighting a holy war that is seen by none but the dead and damned."

The Old Man's voice remained deeply patient, his words practiced, yet delivered with honesty.

"We are brothers, Sons of the Light, fighting against the darkness. We hold the Light, as our Holy Lord did before us. Though the Kings declare *True Peace*, my Brothers, and I have fought an unseen war for many generations. We go now to end that war."

Houst spat over the side again and stared upriver, not flinching as the boat dipped and the river spat back.

"Fighting an unseen war sounds like a better waste of time than some. I'll take you as far as you need, as long as your money's good. And it will be good. You'll be hard-pressed to find another boat that will travel as far. Not many go West of here at all. In fact, with this breeze, we'll be off the charts in two days. I've never been much farther than that. Only a handful of small settlements between us and the mountains."

The boatman nodded to the grey smudge that painted the far horizon, his towel dabbing more sweat as it rolled toward his eyes.

"I asked before, but I'll ask again. How far upriver are you bringing your Lord's steel?"

The Holy Man never took his eyes from the far mountains. When he answered, his deep voice overtook the breeze and bounced off of the banks of the river.

"I don't know. I'm going as far as it takes to complete my purpose. To that end, I would cross the mountains themselves. Men may not move through the West, but the darkness calls it home. With any luck, we'll capture it on the doorstep."

The fat boatman rolled his eyes to the Old Man's back. He shifted in his seat and looked back over his shoulder towards the flat farmlands to the East.

"Well, this breeze won't keep up forever. So, unless your friend is stronger than he looks, I'll only be able to take you so far."

The Holy Man continued to stare West, upriver.

"We'll be stopping to collect more Brothers. Wind be damned. We have the Light, and our Lord calls us upriver."

Houst squirmed back around to spit once more over the side. He dabbed at his glistening brow with his grimy towel. He ended the conversation with a grunt.

"Well... the boat seats eight."

The next day, the vessel rounded another bend in the river, and the Holy Man stood in the belly of the boat, one hand braced against the mast as he peered through the grey fog that had followed them all morning. The breeze at their back was gone now, and their journey slowed to a crawl as the sky above grew darker by the minute. The Holy Man called to his pupil.

"Elias."

At his teacher's word, the young man's eyes snapped open. The Holy Man motioned to the oars, and the sturdy lad immediately took up position in the center of the boat, an oar in each hand. As he pulled against the water, the boat moved against the current, and they were once more making headway upriver. With the rain growing slightly worse, the boatman locked the tiller in place and quickly set about reefing the sail. Soon, it was only the young man's strength that propelled them upstream. Two hours passed, and the lad showed little sign of tiring.

"There!"

The Holy Man's voice was low, his word a barked whisper. The boatman's eyes followed the word through the fog and grey, until the fat man saw the object. In the distance, a great stone bridge spanned the width of the river. The structure was high and long, easily reaching over the waterway and the surrounding floodplain. Two mighty pylons of black stone rose out of the water to hold the structure aloft. Weather and time had worn the dark stone smooth.

As the boat drew slowly closer, a light flickered and then sparked to life atop the bridge. The flame pierced through the grey haze and the Holy Man nodded assuredly.

"Our Brothers have the Light. We will anchor at the bridge. They will accompany us the rest of the journey."

With Elias pulling them upstream, Houst brought the boat up beneath the bridge and anchored her there. The Holy Man crouched near the bow. The torch on the bridge above him was gone. He blinked away the raindrops, neck craned back as he searched the bridge overhead for signs of life.

Shortly, a great coil of rope cascaded off of the Western side of the bridge. With one end secured above, the free end of the rope hit the water, and the current carried it slowly downstream. The fat boatman fished it from the water and fastened it about the stern, near the tiller. The rope began to dance as a figure lowered itself down through the rain, hand over hand, from the bridge above.

As the man set foot on the gunwale, the Holy Man hailed him.

"Is the Light within you?"

The newcomer dropped to the bottom of the boat, grabbing the mast to balance himself. He shrugged off his travel pack and threw back his hood. He smiled up at the Holy Man. His face was distorted with jagged scars and metal piercings.

"The Light is within me, Brother!"

The Holy Man helped the gaunt, scarred fellow to his feet. The rope danced as another figure began to descend. The two Brothers embraced one another briefly about the shoulders. When they parted, the Holy Man spoke first—his words heavy with burden.

"Brother Rhen—most loyal lieutenant. To see you again is to see the war. What news of the North? Have you spread the Light to the wells of the wasteland and the Sand Sea?"

Boots thudded on the planks behind them, and another Son of the Light deposited his pack into the boat. The scarred man shook his head, but allowed his twisted smile to remain.

"The North remains in darkness. But I have news. The True King is dead, and one of his sons has claimed the throne of Vestal!"

As the rest of the Brother Rhen's company slid down the rope, the Holy Man guided his old friend to the bow where they crouched and spoke in hushed tones.

"The True King dead? How long ago did this happen?"

The newcomer wiped rainwater from his scarred face, shrugging slightly.

"Not sure exactly when. I heard just this morning from a rider. Couldn't have been more than three, maybe four days ago. Apparently, most of the kingdom is in an uproar."

The Holy Man was unblinking.

"Uproar? I left the city not two days ago. Surely someone would have heard of the King's death by then?"

Brother Rhen glanced down the length of the boat, nodding to Elias and openly smirking at the fat boatman. He looked back, smiling up at the Holy Man.

"That *city* is just a fishing settlement. No militia, no court, and no shites are given about the King. According to the rider, back in the East, several magistrates have openly refused to recognize the young Prince as a worthy successor. At least one city in the South has revolted and no doubt there will be more to follow."

The Holy Man pressed the issue.

"What of the King's Militia? They may not be in every fishing hut and marketplace, but surely they are still in the cities. They have been called to put down riots in the past, why not now?"

At the mention of the Militia, the lieutenant chuckled.

"The Militia are cowards. I'd give a score of them for one true Believer any day. Also, they are at the call of the King, and no word has come from the King's Hall except that which declared his kingship. Essentially, the Kingdom is on the brink of toppling, and this boy-Prince does nothing. If the Brotherhood had any sense at all, we'd turn the situation in our favor. Now is the time to solidify! If we marched in force on the King's Hall, we could overthrow the boy and his guard and put one of our own in power!"

The Holy Man looked grim.

"That is not our calling. The Brotherhood has been tasked with great purpose in the West. There is darkness and blood there that must be washed with the Lord's Light."

The Brother hissed his dissent.

"There's darkness everywhere, Brother! If we shone the Light in the East, in the King's Hall, we could drive the darkness from every corner of Vestal. We have the might of our Lord at our side! It is his will that we shine the Light, even in the places of power!"

The Holy Man was quiet, but his eyes were smoldering a dark fire. His stare overtook the other man, and Rhen looked shamefully down at the mud on his boots. His tone was once again low, his words carefully chosen.

"I'm sorry, old friend. I know how important our work in the West is to you. I grow excited in the face of opportunity. We will complete our task. I am yours to command."

The grey-haired man blinked, watching his friend closely. The moment passed, and the Holy Man nodded to the messenger bag slung across the newcomer's chest. His voice was softer now, lower than before.

"What news?"

Once again, the scars and piercings made a mockery of the Brother Rhen's smile. He shifted in the bow as the boatman untied the rope from the sternpost and called for the anchor to be drawn in. As the Holy Man's pupil began to row once more, the three fresh recruits joined him. With four able-bodied men at the oars, the small vessel nearly skipped upriver through the rain. The scarred fellow untied the leather thongs on the bag and presented the Holy Man with two letters, both sealed with a dark green wax in the shape of a sunburst.

"I've been in the area for two weeks. These are our scout's reports from the West. They bear your name. One arrived last week, the other, just yesterday. I have not opened them."

The Holy Man broke the seals, and his scarred lieutenant took the moment to fetch his pack and make sure his three comrades were settled. By the time he had returned from the belly of the boat, his elder was reading the reports for a second time. Brother Rhen checked that his pack was secure and his armor and steel were out of the rain. Only after his elder had finished reading the letters did he speak.

"The darkness... It moves in the West?"

The Holy Man sat cross-legged in the bow, hands resting in his lap, his back straight. He stared upriver, West, to the grey mountains in the distance. His voice was low, a rumble of brooding thunder deep within his chest.

"The darkness is there. Several settlements have embraced it in the last months. But we knew this, or we guessed anyway."

The scarred Brother spat against the evil tidings—against evil.

"They have embraced the darkness? We shall bring them the Light, and steel besides!"

The venom in these words was lost on the Holy Man, his weathered hands folding the papers and stuffing them into his own pouch as his mind eased into deep thought.

"It is worse than that. The darkness grows deeper."

The next words slipped out, and Rhen's tone betrayed his fear before he could stop himself.

"The blood?"

Behind the pair, in the belly of the boat, the four other Sons of the Light had grown suddenly quiet. The three newcomers exchanged glances as they strained to hear what was said next. The broad-shouldered Elias sat with his eyes closed, his face as stone, his large chest rising and falling in rhythm with the pulling of the oars. Behind them all, in the stern, the fat boatman gripped the tiller with a grimy hand and slurped from a wineskin. He'd heard nothing, and it was better that way.

Brother Rhen was aware that the others were listening, but his eyes never left the Holy Man. The elder Brother stared at the mountains far upriver. When he spoke, the words weren't directed to the man at his side, but rather, it was as though he was musing aloud.

"We fight an unseen war. Our Kings and Magistrates claim peace where there is none, forcing us to gather in secret. For this, we are unseen. And our enemies, they too gather in secret. Can one truly see the darkness if there is no Light? And now—a cold wind blows. A voice in the darkness. The blood speaks, and we are called upriver."

At the mention of the blood, the scarred man spat at his feet. Two of the eavesdroppers behind mimicked the gesture. The fourth member of their company was shaking, his face pale. The Holy Man's pupil was still as stone. Again, Rhen hissed his fears to his elder.

"A voice? And it said it was from the dark? Claiming the darkness and the blood is a sign of power—demons! And now, a voice is doing just that? How are we, a half-dozen, supposed to cast down the legions of the dark and the blood?"

The Holy Man stood, and the motion was so sudden that the Brother close to his side fell back into the belly of the boat where his scarred face stared up at his elder with awe. The boat pointed West, and the late afternoon sun cut through the grey clouds on the horizon. Beams of sunlight shimmered through the raindrops and mist, silhouetting the Priest as he stood at the bow, a figurehead now facing the six men, all staring up at him.

The Holy Man drew his steel, and the sunlight flashed on the blade. He held it aloft, his hand gripping the edge, the hilt raised above his head. The pommel was inlaid with gold—a sunburst that glinted in the sunlight. His voice was strong and reached into the very hearts of those who heard his words.

"Our Lord has set before us a great quest; to cast down the darkness in this world. This is what we do now. Our task is before us, in the untamed, uncharted lands upriver. The world of men and their civilization may be crumbling behind us, but it matters not. We are Sons of the Holy Lord. It was he that first brought the Light against the darkness and did battle with the blood. Now it is our turn. We bring the Fire and, with it, we will burn the dark and the blood. In his name!"

The men in the boat stared in awe for a moment, and the sunlight in the West faded as the dark clouds closed again. Then the rain fell with earnest.

II

It rained that night and into the next day. The wind became petulant, buffeting from one direction only to turn and blow from another. The four men in the middle of the boat pulled at the oars and the flat-bottomed vessel continued to make headway up the river. Every so often, Brother Rhen would move back and take a turn at an oar but only long enough to give his men a chance to eat a quick bite. The Holy Man remained crouched at the bow unblinking in the steady rain. Elias took no respite and worked at his rowlock through the night.

"He doesn't eat. He doesn't rest. He'll be little use when the fighting starts."

The lieutenant's muttered words brought a frown from the Holy Man. The elder stared at the clouds to the West. They were beginning to shine, as though a bright fire burned in the sky beyond.

"The Light burns in him as true as it burns within me. There is no need for the sustenance of men. We will eat and sleep once our task is finished."

Rhen blinked in the rain as he eyed the Holy Man. After a moment, he nodded toward the clouds ahead and steered the conversation elsewhere.

"Settlement ahead. It's a few miles inland. Last bit of civilization before we wander off the map, as it were. Best place to find information or even good people to give it. Those still loyal to the Brotherhood."

He looked up to the older man, ridged at the bow.

"Will... will we be stopping, then? Not all of the men have your inner-strength. They are not meant—"

The Holy Man's words cut him.

"They are not filled with the Light. I told you to meet me at the bridge. I told you to bring as many true Sons of the Light as you could muster... And you brought me three."

Brother Rhen knelt at the elder's side, water droplets shedding from his piercings as he shook his head. His voice was low, a hiss dampened by the weather.

"Most of the Brotherhood are already in the West! Years of fighting this unseen war have made us weak and our numbers few. I was hard-pressed to find men who knew how to hold steel, let alone ones that would swear to our Lord!"

The Holy Man turned away from the horizon. Rhen cowered under his dark eyes.

"They are without the Light. Without the Light, their words are hollow and their flesh is weak. You speak of the weakness of our Brotherhood and, yet, it is *you* that makes it so! For we are only as strong as the weakest among us, and you have brought sheep to hunt the wolves!"

Rhen tried to plead his case.

"They are no sheep! They are fighters! Seasoned warriors, each of them!"

The Holy Man snorted.

"Whose war did they fight? Some Baron? A Magistrate? And *who* did they fight? Soldiers? Peasants with hay forks? We are delving into the heart of darkness. We go now to battle being whose names are not spoken in this world. When the Light does not show itself within these men, will you be there? What will you do... when you realize that a handful of coins and a few words will not give them the ability to purify the blood and the dark?"

There was silence as the Holy Man turned his gaze back upriver, to the fire in the distant clouds. The bow of the boat jostled the pair as the rowers toiled on through the inclement weather. Brother Rhen kept his head low.

"I have failed you. I let my fear of the darkness cloud my judgement. We do bring sheep to hunt the wolf, and I am one of those sheep."

Despite the lieutenant's admission of guilt, the Holy Man kept his eyes on the horizon. When he spoke, his words were tired.

"The wolf walks in the darkness, my Brother. He seeks to devour us, lest we upset his wicked schemes. And now, we bring the Fire. But we also bring steel. Perhaps even the sheep will have their purpose."

The boat plowed on, and the flames in the clouds grew brighter.

III

Dawn the next morning was grey and grim. At the Holy Man's call, the Boatman, Houst, pulled into the Northern bank. Putrid wetlands and marsh made up the floodplain on both sides of the water, and it took much effort for the men in the boat to remove themselves and find solid footing.

As soon as they were on firm ground, the Holy Man presented them all with a strip of clean, white silk from the depths of his pockets. Each Brother tied a white scarf about his waist. The fresh linen stood out in the grey morning light, the clean white fighting against the blackened muck of the marsh and worn clothes of the Brothers. Rhen ordered one of his men, Brother Carlsten, to stay with the boatman.

"If we come back, and this boat ain't here..."

He left the thought unfinished, speaking to neither man in particular but, rather, directing his voice to the air around them. Carlsten nodded, securing his white scarf about his waist and taking up position in the bow of the boat. The fat man, Houst, dabbed at his face with his dirty towel and gripped the tiller.

The remaining Brothers moved as quickly as they could across the wetlands. A half hour passed before they reached the tree line. They had stripped themselves of blankets, rations, and anything that could be left in the boat, giving them freedom to move quickly and fight unencumbered. The Holy Man went first, the rest following quietly.

Shortly after entering the trees, the moisture in the air began to reek of smoke. The rain had slowed, but the sky was still covered with a heavy blanket of wet, dark grey. Catching a break in the trees, Rhen gestured to a plume of light smoke to the Northwest. They continued through the underbrush for a quarter of an hour before they heard the sound of voices. The Holy Man adjusted course, and they soon stepped out of the woods and onto a small wagon trail. The makeshift road was straight, thin, and mostly mud, but the Brothers ignored this and set their attention on the smoking rubble in the clearing just opposite them.

Judging by the signpost near the road, it had once been an Inn. The roof was burned out and the windows shattered. The blackened stones of the building's foundation marked the edge of the horror. Two men stood in the misty morning air, blinking against the smoke, and clutching shoddy, wooden spears in wet, wrinkled hands. About their waists, the men wore weathered scarves of their own. Perhaps the cloth had once been white but now it was a mottled, dirty grey. At their feet, a half-dozen corpses lay in a tidy row. Several had feathered shafts sprouting up from their chests, another looked to be burned from head to foot.

The men with the crooked, wooden spears chuckled to one another, their backs to the road, their shoulders hunched against the mist. The Holy Man called to the pair, causing them to leave off their conversation and whip around so fast that one of them slipped and fell in the mud.

"Hail Brothers, Sons of our Holy Lord! Do you have the Light?"

The man who had fallen into the muck floundered about, his torn and soaked hood now stuck to his face. The remaining spearman looked from the Holy Man, to the sheathed steel in his hand, to the white scarf at his waist. His reply was a croak, followed by a fit of coughing.

"Aye! We—we have the Light!"

The men in white scarves crossed the mud to the pair and took in the sight of the wreckage more thoroughly. After a moment, their elder turned back and once more addressed the spearmen.

"Who is in charge here?"

The Holy Man nodded to the rubble as he asked his question. The fellow who had remained on his feet brushed wet hair from his face with muddy fingers.

"That would be Brother Liam. He ordered the fire to be lit yesterday morning, but no one could get the thatch to take flame until last night. Once we finished the business, he told us to remain behind and make sure that nothing was left."

Brother Rhen shuffled past them with his scarred face full of piercings and peered into the middle of the smoking, blackened ruin. The lieutenant spat on the ground before turning to the spearman.

"Brother Liam, eh? Where is this Brother Liam now?"

The man glanced briefly at Rhen, but it was the Holy Man's dark eyes that held his attention. He licked his lips and shrugged quickly.

"I don't know. Like I said, he left. He went up the road, but I don't know if he was headed back to the market, or if he was gonna pay the farmhouse a visit."

He nodded up the road to the North. The Holy Man followed the gesture with his gaze, now ignoring the spearman. Rhen shouldered his way past the grey-scarfed men and stood next to his commander. The scarred man coughed against the grey smoke. The elder mused quietly, his voice so low that it nearly stuck to the mud of the road at their feet.

"I've heard of him—Liam. He will know. He's seen the darkness and the effects of the blood. If a voice claimed the darkness here, Liam will know of it. He will hunt down every trace of the dark and bring the Light with him. As always, darkness will flee the Light, and he'll be left with nothing but shadows. Still, a man like Brother Liam will surely know where the voice came from."

The Holy Man stared up the road to where the rain of the grey sky met the dirt below. He raised his voice.

"How far to the farmhouse?"

IV

Smoke of the fire lingered on their wet clothes long after they left the gristly business at the roadside. The weather remained grey and bleak over the next hour as the small company moved North along the road and then West through the trees. Now the ground at their feet was bruised and torn, the branches of the trees around them chopped and broken. It was as though they were following a herd of cattle that had plunged through the undergrowth sometime during the night. Brother Rhen made such a comment, prompting a chuckle from his two men behind. The Holy Man led them in silence, and Elias drove them from behind, his face carved as stone.

The trees and bracken gave way to a clearing—a small pasture with a large farmhouse in the middle. There was a well and several other outbuildings. The grey sky and light drizzle of rain cast a sultry mood over the scene.

A gang of men, perhaps a twenty or more, were assembled in a scattered ring around the farmhouse. Some stood behind sheds and several crouched behind hay bales. All were armed with steel and all had dirty, grey scarves about their waists. Three men with scarves at their hip and steel in their hands stood in the open, a good distance from the others, clearly out of danger. The Holy Man raised his steel, hilt first, into the air above his head. He spoke with authority.

"We bring the Light!"

His words were slightly muffled in the grey mist and wet grass, but every man in the clearing heard them. Several of the encircling troupe shot each other quick glances, but their attention remained fixated on the house. The three men standing away from the others began to move in a wide arc, around the house, along the treeline, eventually reaching the Holy Man and his small band of white scarves.

A short, thick Brother led them. With a sigh, he sunk a cruel looking warpick into the wet earth before pulling back his hood and staring grimly at the newcomers. The stout fellow leaned on the long handle of the warpick and produced a short, clay pipe from his breast pocket. He prodded gently at the contents of the bowl and struck a match. In the damp mid-morning air, it took a moment for him to coax a thick smoke from the stem. His eyes studied the grass around their boots, then their clean, white scarves before looking them in the eyes.

"Well met, my Brothers. I'm called Liam. I am here with a purpose. To scatter the darkness and burn the blood. That is my purpose. For six years, I have served my purpose. North to the sand seas and South to the frozen peaks, I have shone the Light of our Lord. Now, what is *your* purpose in this place, so close to the darkness?"

The Holy Man spoke.

"I received a report from this area. *A voice has claimed the darkness, and it is strong.* What can you add?"

The Brother raised his head and cocked an eyebrow at the Holy Man. He clenched the stem of his pipe between his teeth, his tongue managing to force his words out around the device.

"Add? What would I add? If I had something to add to my own field report I would have put it in there when I wrote the damn thing. *It. Is. Strong.* I said that well enough, didn't I? Usually, darkness flees the Light, and we give chase. A few shadows may remain, but they are easily dissipated. But now... Now, the darkness buries itself in the deepest crevices like a tick on a hound dog."

He lightly spat a speck of burned-out ember from his the tip of his tongue. He wiped the end of the pipe on his own weathered, greying scarf before returning it to his lips. Again, the Brother clenched his teeth as he spoke.

"It's the same shite every year. I ask the Brotherhood to send me more Believers. They don't. I'm forced to make Believers out of the locals. You know what I have to do to get a man to wear the white around here? These boys—"

He motioned over his shoulder with his pipe.

"These boys here, they might never have said the proper words, or been anointed beneath the sacred cathedral, but I'll swear to you that they have seen our Lord's Light closer and brighter than most. Every year, the darkness swarms over this territory. Every year, it slaughters a few head of livestock. Every year, a few people go missing. But this year... This year was different. This year, the darkness started talking to people. A few traders at the market spoke to the darkness. Then those folks down at the Inn let the darkness stay under their roof."

The Holy Man gestured to the farmhouse. "And here?"

Brother Liam was quiet a moment. He studied the sky, puffing his pipe and letting the right thoughts form before daring to open his mouth.

"There's power in words. For a voice to claim the darkness takes practice in a dark craft. Craft of the blood."

The short Brother watched the clouds for another moment. His face was tired, his words were blunt.

"I'll ask again, Brothers. What is your purpose?"

The Holy Man stated his purpose.

"I am here to silence the voice that claims the darkness."

The rain was light but steady. Water mingled with sweat and caused rivulets to run down the faces of the men in the pasture. Brother Rhen brushed water from his scarred cheeks and eyed the farmhouse. His men behind shifted in their soaked boots and gripped their steel. Elias was a stone; the rain fell on him ignored. The Holy Man's words hung in every man's ear.

The short, sturdy fellow let the pipe burn a moment. The smoke snuck up and over the lip of the bowl, wreathing itself about the man's large, swollen knuckles. When Liam finally spoke, his voice sounded warm, as though it carried the mirth that his face did not.

"You're here to silence the voice? That's a damn fine thing. Not many men could boast of having such purpose. I, myself, don't know any such men. However, I've heard of one or two men...

strong, gritty bastards. Real *torches* for the Light that would be bold enough to claim such a goal. It would be a short list I could make for you. And, it's my guess that you'd be... what, top of that list? That, or you wouldn't be here stating such a fine claim. So, top of the list? You're the one they call 'The Teacher'. And, if your reputation is correct, you wouldn't come alone. Not without your trophy. Which would make—"

Liam's eyes left the Holy Man and again searched among the faces of the small group until his gaze fell on the pupil, Elias. He smiled, looking back to the Teacher.

"Him. He's the one, isn't he? The Holy Man and his Holy Fire. Two torches with white scarves on a mission to cut off the serpent's head? End all this, eh?"

Here, Brother Liam jerked his head back over his shoulder, indicating the farmhouse surrounded by his grey scarves. The Holy Man nodded.

Liam's lips smirked as his eyes scanned the sky. It was grey, but the rain was finally letting up. After a moment, he turned and muttered to one of the men at his side. The taller fellow nodded and moved away, heading across the pasture towards a cluster of men who were crouched behind a large apple cart. The grey scarf commander spoke aloud as his boot prodded the earth where he'd lodged the warpick.

"A Brother arrived in the area three weeks ago. Walked out of the West with a scarf so tattered it barely held its shape. He claimed the Light and told us of the coming darkness."

The short man clenched his pipe in his teeth and dug once more into his deep, inner pockets. He grunted as he handed the Teacher a damp, folded letter.

"He also said that you, or someone like you, would come and, when you did, we should give you this. I haven't opened it."

The stout Brother grasped the handle of the warpick in his right hand and kicked at the head of the weapon, knocking it free from the wet ground. The Holy Man stowed the letter in his own pocket. His words were brief.

"Anything else?"

Brother Liam shook his head and shouldered his cruel weapon.

"No, he died later that night. He claimed to hear a voice in the darkness. A week ago, that voice showed itself. More people heard the words it spoke. Some listened."

The Brother stared at the divot in the earth and puffed absently at the pipe, still smoldering in the palm of his left hand. Behind the short man, several grey scarves in the field were busy tearing apart one of the large, round bales of hay that dotted the pasture. They then loaded the dry, inner hay into the back of the apple cart.

"Every shadow left by the darkness is a foothold. We'll soon show them the Light."

The small group watched in silence as the soldiers built a fire in the cart. Once the flames were strong and new tinder had caught fire, the grey scarves quickly wheeled the cart up to the backside of the farmhouse. The thatch was wet from the night's rain, but after several moments of sitting under the flames, it began to send up great billows of smoke. Soon, there was a flicker of flame in the thatch itself, and within moments, thick, white smoke spewed from every crack and crevice of the house. Outside, the men waited with naked steel.

The door opened. A pair of small boys bolted from the cabin, one going left, down the hill for the well house, the other shot right, up the gentle slope towards the tree line. Both stumbled and were caught before getting twenty paces. The grey scarves beat them with the blunt ends of their steel until the pair were unconscious. The door remained open, smoke spewing out of its maw while the men across the pasture watched and waited.

Another figure burst from the doorway. A woman, hair on fire and a woodcutter's axe in her hands, sprinted for the men standing over the two boys. Her awkward rush sent her straight onto the end of a leveled spear. The axe fell from her hands as she writhed and squirmed on the spear's long blade. One of the grey's put an end to her struggle by burying his steel into her neck with both hands.

The man holding the spear shrieked as an arrow from the flaming house caught him in the hip. The rest of the Brothers moved away from the fire, dragging their wounded man and the battered boys with them. No one else ran out of the cabin. Even as it collapsed in on itself and the flames popped and crackled against the moisture.

Brother Liam knocked the last of the embers from his pipe and stowed it. He turned back to face the Holy Man.

"This voice that claims the darkness. Its strength isn't whole yet in these lands. We've seen to that. West. That is where the darkness is thickest.

That is where this voice will be. I have little doubt of that."

He gripped his warpick and set off across the pasture. The stout fellow called over his shoulder as he strode toward the blazing building.

"Farther West, Teacher. Follow the river. Another two, maybe three days... you'll hear the voice soon enough. Light guide you."

Shrieking cries hurtled from the center of the inferno and followed the Holy Man as he led his white scarves once more into the trees, leaving the farmhouse behind.

V

It was midday by the time the Brothers made it back to the boat. The sky was clear, and again, there was a steady breeze coming up the river from the East. The Holy Man called for the sail and moved to his position at the bow. The scarred lieutenant, Rhen, tightened the white scarf about his waist and settled in the belly of the boat by the mast. As the boatman, Houst, maneuvered them toward the middle of the river, he looked to the sun and clear skies above and called out to the Holy Man.

"Looks like you brought the light after all, my friend. I take it your foray inland went well?"

The Holy Man was silent. The scarred fellow in the belly of the boat grinned up at Houst, his piercings glinting in the high sunlight.

"No need to pry, boatman. West. Upriver."

Houst dabbed sweat with his towel and squinted in the sun.

"Don't mean to pry. Just don't want to end up dead is all. Too far West and a man will find himself witness to things best left to campfire stories."

Brother Rhen spat at his feet.

"This is no campfire story. If the darkness scares you, then you shall always be afraid. Darkness is in the mountains, but it is here as well. We'll all die one day, boatman. That much is certain."

The lieutenant looked to the bow. The Holy Man sat with the letter given him by the grey scarfed commander. Behind him, the broad-shouldered pupil sat with his arms folded, eyes closed. The scarred fighter picked at one of the piercings in his lip.

"Well, for most of us, it's certain."

The breeze carried them for two days. The river was wide and slow, and the flat-bottomed boat skimmed along the surface, moving ever further West. The Brothers in the belly of the vessel slept and talked among themselves. The Holy Man stared upriver and read the worn letter many times. His pupil crouched at his feet and breathed slowly, his face a blank slate. The fat boatman, Houst, didn't sleep. Each night, he packed a pinch of brown leaf into his cheek and spat juices over the side as he steered the boat ever upriver. Come morning, his face was stained and his eyes were dark.

"I'll not trust my boat in the hands of an ill-experienced man."

By the morning of the third day, the fat fellow was a wreck. His sweat towel was a moist pile on the deck, and the gunwale next to his elbow was awash with brown mucus. He stared at the riverbank as it moved past. The wide marshland gave way to tall trees, their roots a tangle of thick brush and undergrowth that obstructed the view from the river. The quiet mood on the boat was shattered by a cry from the bow.

"Behold, the darkness!"

The Holy Man stood, his arm outstretched. The Brothers in the belly of the boat all strained to get a look at the sight upriver. The pupil, Elias, opened his eyes and looked. The scarred man clutched his steel.

"Light hold us all..."

The river ahead split, one arm bending around to the North, the other continuing on towards the Western mountains. Between the arms of the fork, an island of tall, moss-covered rocks and stunted evergreens sprang sharply out of the midst of the river. There, high above the water, suspended like a giant spider between two pine trees was a sodden, torn figure. Ropes bound his outstretched arms and legs, his head hung limp against his chest. About his waist, a tattered and bloodied grey scarf spat about on the morning breeze.

The men in the boat sat in silence as the wind drew them near. The bow pushed into the large, swirling eddies caused by the gentle currents meeting in front of the island. The boatman called for the anchor to be thrown over. The Holy Man was over the side, sheathed steel gripped in his right hand as he waded to the rocky bank, Elias close at his side.

Rhen barked, and the rest of the Brothers were soon over the rail, white scarves dragging through the water, naked steel in their hands. Looking back to the vessel, Rhen shouted over the swirling water.

"Brother Trent, stay with the boatman! Don't let him leave!"

At the scarred lieutenant's order, the man nearest the boat turned back and hauled himself over the gunwale, but he needn't have bothered. Houst sat over the tiller, his eyes locked on the figure suspended above. The boatman clutched an uncorked wineskin in his hand, and a stream of brown dribble flowed from the corner of his mouth. He wasn't going anywhere.

The Holy Man and his pupil were the first ones out of the water, but it was Brother Ernst, the youngest of the party, that first reached the high ground overlooking the river. The undergrowth and smaller, stunted trees had all been cleared away, leaving the pair of pines alone on the rocky outcropping. As they arrived on the spot, the Brothers circled the suspended figure, their eyes watching the banks across the river below and the forest behind, every now and then glancing at the body above.

Elias stood as a statue, looking up at the face of the figure. The Holy Man stood next to him. While the Brothers watched the trees around, the pair held communion.

"It is as I believed. The voice speaks, and the darkness answers."

The Teacher's words were a sigh. He glanced at his pupil, but the lad was silent. The elder Brother continued his thought.

"This is the beginning of the end. We bring the Light, but in this place, the darkness swallows the Light."

Elias stared at the hanging figure, his face as stone—gaze unblinking. The Holy Man closed his eyes, lifting his face to the sky above.

"But now, I've brought the Fire. This darkness will not swallow us. No. It will be consumed."

The sun hung in the clear, mid-day sky, the river moved slowly past the outcropping, and the Brothers waited. After a time, the Teacher opened his eyes. As the older man stepped away, the lieutenant nodded and called to his subordinates, Brothers Carsten and Ernst.

"Cut the poor fellow down. Dig a trench and bury the body."

As the men moved to follow orders, the Holy Man spoke.

"No. We don't have time to bury him. We must get back to the boat and continue. For now, wrap him in a cloak and sink him in the river. When we come back this way, we'll have time to dispose of him properly."

The youngest Brother, Ernst, shimmied up the Northern tree, a knife in his belt, his hand grasping for the rope binding the corpse. The scarred lieutenant spoke up again.

"Brother, it won't take long to dig a trench. If we sink him in the river, the fish will have at him. We should bur—"

The Holy Man cut him off, his voice suddenly sharp.

"No! Do as I say! This is the doorstep of the darkness, and we haven't the time—"

There was a flopping crash as Ernst cut the rope, and the body of the grey scarf smashed into the ground between the Holy Man and his lieutenant. Though they were somewhat startled, neither moved until the young Brother in up in the tree cried out.

"The boat! The boat!"

Sure enough, as the men on the hill ran to the edge of the rocks, the boat was just moving away from the bank below them. Rhen barked an order and darted down the rocks, Carlsten and Ernst close at his heels. Elias and the Holy Man remained behind. The old man watched the boat, but the broad-shouldered lad's attention was still fixed on the body that had fallen from the trees.

Within a minute, the boat was well downriver, twisting awkwardly in the current. Before the vessel was out of sight around the bend, the lieutenant had returned to the outcropping, his chest heaving as he gave the Holy Man his report.

"The boatman is dead. His guts are in the river."

Brother Rhen stared at the Holy Man, his jaw quivering as he spoke.

"The darkness is here."

VI

The boatman was dead. Brother Trent, the man left to guard him, was found soon after. His mangled body was farther up the Northern fork of the river. His face was purple, nearly black, his neck broken. With no boat to take them upriver, the Holy Man no longer objected to a burial. Two trenches were dug on the hilltop above, and the bodies of the Brothers were put to rest. Rhen rolled the fat boatman's corpse into the river. He spat after the body as it bobbed and sank under the current.

"It was him that let the darkness so close. Never should have let an outsider come this far along with us."

The Holy Man watched as the surviving Brothers placed dirt and rocks over their fallen comrades. The Teacher shook his head and glanced at the sun. It was nearly noon. The Holy Man turned away as Brother Rhen set about marking the two graves with steel. The elder joined his pupil at the Northern bank. The younger man stared past the slow-moving waters to the forest on the other side. His eyes shifted among the trees, probing the distant silence with his own.

The Holy Man followed the direction of his gaze and spoke softly.

"We are in the darkness, now. But we bring the Light. We mustn't fade or falter."

The Holy Man turned to Elias. His dark eyes searched the young man's face; his brow furrowed momentarily.

"To silence the voice, we must first hear it speak. Will you know the voice when you hear it?"

The pupil didn't answer. His eyes stopped their shifting, his face once again as stone. The Holy Man stared at the water moving past them. Brother Rhen finished his words over the shallow graves. He and his two remaining compatriots gathered their steel— as it was all they had taken from the boat. The three approached the elder. Rhen spoke, his voice raised as to be heard over the river.

"We've come this far, Holy Man. One of our number lies buried, and another Brother besides. This is the work of the darkness, no mistake. We're bound by the words to bring the Light. Well, we're here. We must find whatever did this. We must silence this... voice."

The scarred lieutenant gripped his steel and glanced to his two men. The young Brother Ernst shifted from foot to foot, licking his lips and refusing to meet Rhen's eyes. Brother Carlsten was grim, his eyes fixed on Elias, his chest rising and falling steadily. Brother Rhen spat on the ground in front of him, looking up at the broad-shouldered pupil but addressing the Holy Man.

"Time for your dog to do his trick."

The Holy Man looked at the ground, at the mucus ejected from Brother Rhen's mouth. The river behind him roared into the swelling silence. When he raised his eyes, the lieutenant and his comrades shifted their footing and gripped their steel closer. The Holy Man's words were sharp.

"You came this far because you claim the Light. If you are true Believers, death is your ultimate reward. To call this man a dog is to spit in the eye of our Lord himself. He has no trick. He is the Fire."

Brother Rhen and his fellows held their ground a moment longer but then quailed away from the pair, moving to stand by the twin pines that had held the grey scarf aloft. The Holy Man watched them move off and then turned to look at his ward. Elias had ignored the encounter, and, with the spark in his eye, he continued to stare North, across the river.

Several hours passed. The five remaining Brothers stood atop the river-island, waiting for a sign from their Lord.

Night fell, and a series of cries rose up from the far bank, howls and screeching that sent the blood pounding through the hearts of the men on the island. Brother Carlsten and young Ernst brandished their naked steel and stared into the darkness, their breath suddenly heavy. The Holy Man stared upriver, his gaze following the sound. Rhen stared up into the night sky, his steel whistling through the air as he prepared himself for the unseen horror.

"So, the darkness comes to snuff out the Light, and my steel will have a chance to speak before we meet our Lord."

The cries from the river reached a crescendo of howling, animalistic wailing—a chorus of otherworldly voices screaming out in pain, lusting for blood. Elias stood at the edge of the hill, staring down toward the darkness on the riverbank, his gaze unblinking. The Holy Man sat at the feet of his pupil, eyes closed, his sheathed steel cradled in his arms. Behind the pair, Rhen and the two Brothers took no solace in the Holy Man's relaxed state.

Suddenly, young Brother Ernst brandished his steel and went charging into the darkness of the riverbank below, a scream tearing at his throat. His cries joined those of the darkness. The lieutenant called after him but to no avail. A few moments later, the screaming night went silent. The Holy Man sighed and bowed his head over his sheathed steel. Rhen spat into the darkness as Carlsten prayed quietly.

The Brothers on the hilltop numbered four.

Dawn revealed a grey sky and brought a curse from Brother Rhen. The man's scarred face hung long as his sleepless eyes searched the far bank.

"We will die here. We should leave. Downriver we can find food and rest. Our allies are there."

The Holy Man rose from his place of meditation. His dark eyes stared into Rhen's and shook the Brother's core.

"Turn back, and we become the darkness. The only way is on. We have brought the Light. Now we must see the deed done."

With these words, they waited.

Another hour passed before Elias shifted from the hilltop. He made his way down and over the sharp rocks of the island and toward the Northern arm of the river. The Teacher followed, his sheathed steel held firm in one hand, the hilt above his head. Lieutenant Rhen and Brother Carlsten were swift to follow.

The party was soon in the river. Cold water pushed over their knees, the current tugging at the white scarves about their waists. At the deepest point, the lieutenant's scarred chin brushed the water, but only for a moment. Soon, the four were across the river and on the far bank.

Dried bracken and pine needles carpeted the forest floor between the trunks of mighty evergreens. The young man spent no time on the bank of the river. The Holy Man caught his breath for a moment before following his pupil North and then West. Rhen and Brother Carlsten loped after them, their bellies rumbling, and their clothes still dripping from the river.

It was well past noon before Elias stopped. There was a break in the trees, and a small clearing opened before them. The young man stood at its center with eyes closed, his head tilted back. The Holy Man sat near the lad's feet, his steel once more cradled in his arms. He too closed his eyes and breathed deep. Brother Rhen clawed his way through the final bit of bracken and collapsed on the mossy ground, his naked steel clenched in his hand. His breath came in huge, tearing gasps as the last of the party crashed through the tree line behind him.

"Where does he take us? There are no signs, no tracks to follow."

The Holy Man looked up at Elias. In the center of the clearing, with the sun breaking through the clouds, the broad-shouldered young man could have been a statue from some age long forgotten. He was silent. He was still.

The Holy Man looked at Brother Rhen.

"He takes us to the voice that claims the darkness. A voice does not leave a trail. It can only be heard."

The teacher looked back to his pupil, his eyes searching the younger man's face.

"He listens."

The scarred lieutenant spat in the dirt and flopped over onto his back, still seeking to calm his racing heart. Behind him, Brother Carlsten didn't move, but his pitiful panting could be heard by all those within the small clearing.

An hour or more passed. The Holy Man remained seated at the foot of his pupil, his steel sheathed, his eyes watching the sun overhead. Elias remained, still as stone. Across the clearing, Rhen scratched at his face and licked his lips, his back to the pair of them. The scarred Brother didn't look round but managed a dry swallow before addressing the old man.

"Your dog hear anything yet?"

The Holy Man remained silent. Rhen snorted and spat a mist through dry lips. Brother Carlsten, the remaining white scarf, was on his feet. He paced the edge of the tree line, his eyes darting between the trunks and branches of the thick forest. Brother Rhen watched him from his seat with hollow interest. It was only when Carlsten stepped out of the clearing and into the trees that the lieutenant spoke.

"Where are you going?" he asked with a dry, choked gasp.

Brother Carlsten didn't turn, didn't stop, but called over his shoulder.

"Water."

The Brother's white scarf was soon lost in the darkness of the underbrush. Brother Rhen stared after him for a moment before glancing back to the Elias and the Holy Man. His words were flat and dull in the small clearing.

"He's going to die out there."

The trees around them sighed as the breeze overhead rippled through the branches. Other than the wind's movement through the pines, there was no sound to be heard. Not one squirrel clawed its way up a tree trunk. Not a single bird called out. Even Brother Carlsten's footsteps were lost after a few short moments. The sun hung overhead, and the three remaining men joined the silence. Carlsten didn't return.

Hours passed, and the sun was behind the treetops when Elias finally moved. Without a word, the young man opened his eyes, stepped across the mossy ground, and plunged once more into the trees. The Holy Man rose to his feet and followed his pupil without a word. Brother Rhen watched the pair begin to melt away through the trees. He managed to spit on the ground as he pulled himself upright and shambled after them.

It hadn't been more than an hour before they found Carlsten. The Brother was dead, his body suspended in the trees like the poor bastard on the river. The scarf had been taken from his waist and knotted about his neck as a noose. His eyes were gouged out. Blood poured forth from the empty sockets, running down the man's face to stain the white scarf about his neck.

Elias halted before the spectacle, his eyes taking in every detail. Behind him, the Holy Man sighed, bowing his head. It was Brother Rhen that spoke. Last through the brush, he came upon the scene and immediately cried out.

"Animals! Bastards! The Light burn them all and send them back to the beginning!"

The lieutenant fell to his knees, flecks of white spittle showed at the corners of his mouth, and his scarred face distorted further as he screamed in wounded agony. His chest rose and fell rapidly as his shock was replaced by anger. He punched the loamy ground with his fist and groaned between clenched teeth as he fought to control his rage.

The Holy Man watched the display with unflinching eyes, his sheathed steel still cradled in one arm. Elias stared upward into the hollow, bloody sockets of the man hanging above them. After a time, Rhen got to his feet, his eyes bloodshot, his lips cracking. The lieutenant gathered himself together before offering an observation.

"Where is his steel?"

The Holy Man augmented the remark.

"The ground is undisturbed. No broken branches, no loose soil."

Brother Rhen shook his head.

"There was no fight."

The trees sighed, and the branches shifted. The body swayed. The forest was silent. Elias cut off his gaze and moved away through the trees. The Holy Man followed. Brother Rhen protested.

"We must cut him down. We must bury him."

The Holy Man was blunt.

"They have taken his eyes—he is without the Light."

VII

It was late afternoon, and the dense, overgrown forest, full of deadfalls and undergrowth, had slowly disappeared, giving way to great oak trees, each rising from the ground to stand as a colossal monument to forgotten nature. The treetops created a thick canopy that filtered the sunlight of its color, leaving the woodlands an empty and grey place. The forest floor was sloped, and the three remaining Brothers of the Light found themselves moving down and deeper into the ever-darkening area.

The three men moved wordlessly through the forest. Brother Rhen stumbled along, his ragged breathing overpowering any sounds the empty woodland should have made. The scarred lieutenant pulled himself after his comrades, his swollen tongue and cracked lips cursing the darkness of their descent. Ahead of him, the Holy Man kept an even, steady pace. He clasped his sheathed steel in his right hand, the sunburst on the hilt raised high over his head as he soldiered on. The broad-shouldered Elias led the party, and the longer they moved, the wider the gap between the lad and the others became.

As darkness fell on the forest, the ground underfoot flattened out and began to make sucking, squelching sounds with each step of the small troupe. Elias halted in his tracks. He stood, his cloak draped about his shoulders, his eyes once more closed to the world around them. Upon reaching his pupil, the Holy Man knelt on the wet ground, planting his steel, point first, in the earth before him. Several moments of silence passed before Brother Rhen reached them. The worn man cast aside his naked steel and prostrated himself on the ground, his lips slurping at a muddy puddle left behind by Elias' bootheel.

Night was upon them. The Holy Man bowed his head and recited quiet prayers. Brother Rhen managed to pull himself up against a tree, his steel once more clenched in his hand, his breath coming easier. Elias was a silent stone.

The forest was quiet and the darkness came and went. The sun rose, its light once again filtered by the tree canopy overhead but now blocked by a thick morning fog. The Holy Man raised his head, his eyes blinking away a fitful moment of sleep. He looked to his pupil. The young lad stood with his eyes still closed, his chest rising and falling slowly as he listened to the woods around them. The Holy Man turned to his lieutenant.

Brother Rhen sat against a nearby oak tree. His eyes were open, unblinking. His belly was bare to the morning air, his exposed entrails spread about the forest floor, a ghastly web of horror and gore. As the Holy Man looked on, the scarred man's face twitched and twisted, his eyes glazing over as his last breath passed his lips to mingle with the steam rising from his open guts.

The Holy Man looked to Elias, now towering over him, a statue silhouetted against the morning's grey light. The old man's voice was dry and broken.

"The darkness is upon us. The voice speaks to you. Will I hear it also?"

He received no answer. As the Holy Man got to his feet, the silent sentry set off through the morning mist, the soggy ground slurping as it pulled at his boots. The old man cradled his sheathed steel in his arms once more and moved after him, taking a last look at Brother Rhen before the fog consumed him.

The Holy Man kept pace with his pupil. As morning passed, the mist vanished and the pair plodded on through the grey woods. The trees thinned out and then disappeared, the putrid soil and muck about their ankles formed into a bog. Their progress slowed, and as the day wore on, the air became thick and heavy. The smell of rot and death seeped through the earth below them. Still, the two men moved onward.

The Holy Man felt solid ground beneath his feet for the first time that day. He looked up and froze in his place. Elias stood just ahead of him. The young man had finally stopped moving.

In the silence of the swamp, a sea of dead creatures stretched out under the grey sky. Thousands of reptiles, rodents, and amphibians littered the earth—split open and drained of fluids. Dotted about the gristly sea, the larger mammals stuck out, shipwrecks on the ocean floor. All the life of the swamp and the forest, their mouths open, screamed in protest at the gruesome silence. Maggots ate the hides and eyes of some but others were fresh, their blood still seeping down into the black muck of the bog. Carrion birds and wild dogs had found the scene; their bodies lay among the rest of the carnage.

The Holy Man's dark eyes opened to the scene, the silence and horror of the sight rushing in like a flood, drowning his senses. His heavy words broke the silence.

"The blood."

Elias said nothing. The young man looked above, past the sea before them. Far in the distance, set atop a hill, an island in the slaughter, there was a pair of grass hovels. His eyes sparked at the sight. The pupil turned and looked down to the Teacher beside him. The old man, his sheathed steel clutched in his weathered hands, locked eyes with Elias. His words were still heavy, but now his voice felt the weight, cracking slightly under the pressure of the sea around them.

"You hear the voice. It has brought us here. The blood is real. This is the heart of the darkness. Tell me, speak to me... Have I brought the Light? Will the Fire burn this place?"

Elias stared into the dark eyes for a moment. The young man blinked and looked back across the sea to the island in the distance. The Holy Man bowed his head. Tears welled up, dripping from his dark eyes to mingle with the bloody muck at their feet.

The pupil set off, the weight of his step smashing the bones and flesh of the sea of creatures. Looking up, the Teacher watched him move. His weathered hands gripped the sheathed steel tight against his chest. After a moment, he followed the young man. As he navigated around the rotting flesh and putrid corpses of deer, moose, and a few bear, the Holy Man's tears poured openly down his face. His hands shook as they reached out in front of him, the hilt of his steel held before his face, an invisible shield to the sight of the carnage around them.

The silence was broken. Their booted feet continued to squelch in the bloody muck, sometimes snapping bones. The Holy Man's breathing intensified, mumbled prayers mixed with muted sobs. In this way, the pair crossed the ocean of red, black, and rot.

It was nearly an hour before they drew near the hill with the grass hovels. As the hillock rose above his head, the Holy Man saw through his tears that a great host of figures had formed around them. Rising out of the bloody sea and emerging from piles of corpses were dozens of men and women, their skin stained with the blood of the hellscape. Their hair was matted and rotting, eyes dark and unblinking, jaws locked firm. Several wore scarves about their waists, dyed black with the blood. The devils formed a ring around the outsiders. Elias halted at the foot of the hill, and the Holy Man stopped as well, his whimpered prayers the only sound on the sea.

The bloody bodies around them watched in silence as Elias and the Holy Man stood at the bottom of the hill. After a time, the young man stepped forward. The horde of ghouls parted, and the broad-shouldered Son of the Light moved past them. As Elias started up the hill, the crowd closed the circle and began to inch inward. The Teacher gripped his steel by the hilt, drawing the blade from the sheath, which he cast aside into the sea. He brandished the steel as the horde surged forward.

"I am Amos. I am a Son of the Holy Lord—and I bring the Light!"

As Elias approached the largest grass hut, there was a squeal from down the hill as the Holy Man opened the chest of the closest devil. The crowd rushed in, and the young man stepped through the doorway into the darkness.

VIII

"Elias."

The voice called to him from the back of the hut. The young man waited in the shadow of the doorway. There was no sound within the darkness for some minutes. When it spoke again, the voice was low, sweeping through the room like thick, black smoke.

"Would you honor me so? I am nothing but a sound in the dark... but you—you are the beacon, the Fire, the warm Light that civilized humanity clings to in their desperation. I am a pauper and you are a King, yet here you are... But not to burn me away. No, not to burn me away."

Elias stepped deeper into the darkness. Taking a breath, he closed his eyes and lifted his face toward the roof of the rotting grass structure. The voice moved closer, a raspy, probing whisper in the silence of the hovel.

"You honor me. Why? It can't be the war. Without the war, there would be no firebrands to your Lord. Your Light would fade. You need the war as I need the blood. So, what great thing has brought you from your throne?"

Elias' face twitched, the stone of his blank expression cracking. The voice darted forward, a lonely child eager to question a new companion.

"Do you dream? I do. I have seen you in my dreams. I saw you in the boat. I saw you on the river. The Teacher brought you to burn away the darkness, but the blood gives me dreams, and the blood tells me you didn't come to burn away the darkness. You are the Fire, but you're not here to destroy. No. You're here for my dreams."

There was a pause, a moment of silent blackness. There was disappointment, self-pity.

"That's why you've honored me... You can hear him, but you can't see him. I can see him—the blood gives me dreams."

The voice was hot with fever, marooned on the island in the sea of blood. Elias felt the voice at his ear, dripping honey and acid.

"The blood can give you dreams. It will show you what you seek. Would you like to see the grey one? He is strong. He doesn't know it; no, he doesn't know it. The grey will bring about great things. The darkness will spread; the Light will burn bright. These things will happen. I have seen them—the blood gives me dreams."

Elias listened, and the silence within the room consumed him. The grasses that made up the walls and roof were black with rot, the air in the enclosed space an oven of disease and death. The voice waited in the silence, allowing the young man to exist and remain in the darkness. After a time, the voice relaxed, retreating back into the depths of the hut, the feverish tones now replaced with quiet confidence.

"No. You will not be tempted with the blood. The dreams are not meant for you. They are mine. That is why you are here. You have come for my dreams."

The young man in the white scarf slowly bowed his head. The voice scoffed.

"You are strong. The darkness is stronger. The blood is stronger still. But you know this; you come to me—into my heart. You seek out the power of the blood. Of course, you realize that I'll not give you aid without price."

Elias listened. The voice chuckled, evoking a rasping cough that suffocated in the thick air of the hovel.

"You must need this boy, this *grey one*. He is very powerful indeed, if you are willing to come here alone—knowing that I will demand my own price for my dreams—knowing that you'll be aided by the blood. Yet still... you come. Surely, you know that this forces me to make my price the highest. You will pay it, else, you wouldn't have come. In short, Elias... your silence is my delight."

The silence was immense, pounding in Elias' ears, swelling and expanding, nearly threatening to burst from the small hut in an explosion of fury. The voice basked in the sound, only destroying it with a whisper once it was sated.

"I will dream for you. I will find this boy of power, this grey one. It's a good thing you brought the Holy Man. The blood will need his eyes. The eyes of a Holy Man are one of the most powerful things in this world. Something tells me that you knew this—but that's no matter to me. What does matter is my price."

Silence flooded the hut, drowning both Elias and the voice on the island amidst the sea of blood. When the voice finally spoke, his whisper was but a soft breath in the young man's ear.

"My price is blood. Yes—blood for dreams. First, I will require your blood; I trust you'll understand. However, the richer part of my price is the blood of the grey one, when you do find him. You will give me his blood, and I will use it."

Elias opened his eyes. He agreed.

The blood of the last true believer splashed into the sea.

The darkness grew, and the Light dimmed.

ABOUT THE AUTHOR

James Gagnon grew up in the State of Maine under the shadow of Stephen King and Mt. Katahdin. As a young chap, he spent countless hours reading the works of Michael Crichton, J.R.R. Tolkien, and Brian Jacques. At the age of twenty, he began writing stories of his own—always dreaming that one day he would be good enough to show others what was in his mind's eye. It wasn't until his daughter was born, ten years later, that he realized his words would never be perfect, and decided to publish his first set of stories—warts and all.

Printed in Great Britain
by Amazon

52383530R00104